ROAST EGGS

ROAST EGGS

A RED BADGE NOVEL OF SUSPENSE

Douglas Clark

Dodd, Mead & Company • New York

1 2 3 4 5 6 7 8 9 10

Library of Congress Cataloging in Publication Data

Clark, Douglas.
Roast eggs.

I. Title.
PR6053.L294R6   1981   823'.914   81-7850
    ISBN 0-396-08004-9   AACR2

For Patricia

CHAPTER I

"Do you remember how old I am, James?"

Angela Connal asked the question without looking at her husband who was sitting across the breakfast table from her. She herself was not eating. She was still busy with her morning post. A glass of warm milk—in a silver beaker-holder—stood by her empty plate, and a brown bottle of parti-coloured capsules lay on its side among the already opened envelopes and their scattered contents.

James Connal, who had reached the toast and marmalade stage, looked across at her and replied: "Drink your milk, Angel, and go back to bed for a couple of hours."

"Don't treat me like a neurotic half-wit, James. I asked you a question. Please answer it."

The little breakfast room was nothing more than an extension of the kitchen. As if to remind them that she was present and could overhear the conversation, Mrs King, the housekeeper, rattled a frying pan on the stainless steel draining board. Neither husband nor wife paid the slightest heed. James Connal continued to look across at his wife. There was no doubt about her beauty. She looked frail, but she had always chosen to wear colours that seemed to enhance her fragility. Her hair was fair, very fair, almost ash-blonde. She was finely made, with no high colouring in her cheeks. The very pale pink of the negligee she was wearing heightened the impression of a soft, yielding delicacy that needed protection, cosseting even, if it were not to wither completely.

After the pause for collecting his thoughts, Connal replied, rather heavily, with a pomposity and precision that obviously irritated his wife: "As it isn't your birthday—today being May 7th and your anniversary being in November—I assume there is something more pertinent behind your question than a mere desire to

7

test my memory. But just to show I am not dodging the issue, and that I really do remember how old you are, I will give you a straight answer. You are thirty-four years and six months."

"And do you consider that to be terribly old for a woman?" It was asked naively—almost a little girl's question, but with the saccharin sweetness of a courtesan who is well aware of the answer and knows she is on safe ground.

Connal ignored the tone and answered factually: "By terribly old, I suppose you to mean past her prime. The answer you want is no. And it is the correct one—not flattery. The pundits—and now I'm approaching forty I count myself one of them—say that a woman is at her best in the decade between thirty and forty." He lifted the percolator and poured himself another cup of black coffee before continuing. "But why the need to bolster your ego—at breakfast of all times?"

She half turned from him to look through the open window. It was the sort of morning that has caused to be written verses of the "Oh, to be in England" variety. The garden said the world was good: the morning sun agreed. Angela allowed her husband just enough time to sweeten and stir the coffee, then, as he raised the cup to his lips, she said quietly. "I was wondering why you have chosen a woman ten years younger than me as your mistress."

Connal spluttered and put the cup down with a crash into its saucer. "Hell! That's coffee all over my knee, and it's hot."

She glanced round at him. "You're over-reacting, as usual, James."

Her husband had pushed the chair back and was on his feet using his napkin on his trousers. "Reacting? Of course I'm reacting to an accusation of having a mistress. I haven't got a mistress."

"This letter says you have."

"What bloody letter? Here, let me look."

She snatched it from the table as he stretched out to take it. "No. I'll hang on to it if you don't mind."

"What the hell does it say?"

"I'll read it to you as you finish mopping your trousers. It is very informative and quite courteous. . . ."

"For God's sake, Angela, is this some sort of sick joke?"

"My correspondent says: 'Dear Mrs Connal, I think you might like to know that the name of your husband's mistress is Elizabeth Leacholt. She is dark-haired and nice-looking, with a very good figure, and she is at least ten years younger than you are!'"

Again there was the sound of movement and activity at the kitchen sink made—or so it seemed—deliberately, to draw attention to the fact that there was a third person present. Mrs King was indicating that the scene was by now definitely embarrassing her. But neither of the protagonists appeared to notice. Certainly not Connal, who flung the stained napkin on to the table and sat down heavily. His body seemed to have shrunk considerably. His cheeks, redder than usual, shone glossily, the skin highlighted by a perfect shave and subsequent cosmetic applications.

"I see. And who is your very informative and quite courteous friend?" The question was a sneer.

"That's just the trouble. I don't know. A pity whoever wrote it didn't sign it. All works of art are so much more valuable when signed, don't you think?"

"So it's anonymous! I might have guessed. Fixit instead of pinxit!" He seemed to reassume his former bulk as relief pumped through his body.

"You haven't denied Miss Leacholt—at least I take it she is Miss, otherwise you could have an outraged husband on your tail."

"I know neither the woman nor the name."

"And you haven't got a mistress?" It was a statement in the form of a question to which she already knew the reply. A reiteration of his former assertion.

"Of course I haven't. If I had, wouldn't you be the first to know? Wives are supposed to cotton on to that sort of thing immediately."

She lifted the glass to sip delicately at its bland contents. "Not this wife, apparently." She put down the milk and paused to shake out of the bottle a small green and black capsule. She put it slowly into her mouth and washed it down with another sip of the milk. "But I've probably been a little slow in the uptake. Due, no doubt to the fact that you haven't exactly overwhelmed me with amorous attention these last few years."

9

"And whose fault is that?" He pushed his plate with the uneaten toast away from him. "Ever since Robin died you've shown no interest in being a wife. You've been introspective. Secretive, even. You haven't wanted me."

"It sounds as if you were concocting the perfect excuse for taking a mistress."

Hands flat on the table, he leant forwards to give emphasis to his words. "Angela, I swear to you I haven't got a mistress. Since I first knew you I've never taken more than a passing interest in any other woman."

"Passing?" She was still speaking quietly, very composedly. "How short-lived is passing? A day? A week? A month. . . ?"

He sat back, exasperated. "You know very well what I mean. I'm a male. If I see an attractive female, I'm interested. I may even ogle her, but it doesn't mean I get as far as even talking to her, let alone making her my mistress."

She replied with exaggerated reasonableness. "But you will agree that my informant must be very sure of his or her ground to be able to go as far as to name the other woman. Nobody just conjures up a name like Elizabeth Leacholt."

"And there's no smoke without fire! I know!"

"I thought that letters like these, if they were just sent to make mischief, purposely omitted names in the hope of keeping the recipient guessing or, alternatively, to cause her to suspect in turn each of her husband's female acquaintances. In that way, one missive can do the maximum damage. But my correspondent has not sought to destroy any other relationships. He—or she—is obviously intent on giving me information, and not on causing mischief for others. I call that a kindly gesture."

"Kindly? Whoever wrote that letter—and a pretty gutless type he must be to send anonymous filth like that—is assuredly intent on causing mischief. He must be, because there is not a shred of truth in the information he has sent you. That means he has conjured it up. And what other purpose could there be for such an invention, if not to cause trouble?"

She appeared to relent slightly. "I should like to believe you entirely, James. I do half believe you . . ."

"Half?"

". . . simply because I dislike the thought of receiving anonymous letters."

"Not because you know me, have been married to me for more than ten years?"

She leaned back in her chair and eyed him critically. "It is precisely because I know you so well that I cannot wholly believe you."

Connal puffed out his cheeks in indignation. "What was that? Because you know me. . . . When have I ever lied to you?"

"As far as I know, never. You are too clever. But I am certain you have seriously misled me on a number of occasions. Over big things."

He said stiffly: "Though I have offered it whenever I thought it necessary, I have never insisted that you should take my advice."

"I wasn't thinking of advice, particularly. But as you have mentioned it, I think I need some now. But not from you, James. Legal advice. I shall call on Henry Latham."

He was disparaging. "All Latham will be able to tell you is that you haven't got a leg to stand on. Anonymous letters just don't count in law."

"We shall see." She picked up her milk again. "Isn't it time you changed your suit and got to the office? Remember the good example you so assiduously set the employees by always being in a minute or two before time."

As he got to his feet she added: "I shall ask Henry to see me at half-past ten—before my hair appointment."

He left the breakfast room without replying. His wife got to her feet and collected his dirty plate and cup before going through to the kitchen.

"I'm sorry, love. I did try to remind you I was here," said Mrs King, her motherly face showing a deal of distress.

"I heard you," said Angela quietly.

"Then why. . . ?"

"I think I wanted you to overhear what was said. You're very kind and discreet, Kingy, and I think, deep down, I wanted you to know. Letting you hear was like talking it over with somebody else—a sort of relief."

"It's a relief to me, too, to hear you say that, lovey. But this business . . ."

"It's all right, Kingy. I'll see Mr Latham. He'll advise me what is best to do."

Latham's office was above a greengrocer's shop in Elmhurst—a narrow door, a narrow stairway and a narrow landing giving on to fairly spacious rooms. They were all well decorated, but looked very much second-best, as though they were only a stopgap arrangement while custom-built premises were being completed elsewhere. But the firm in which Latham was a partner had been in these same offices since the First World War. The partnership had been planted, had taken root and then had burgeoned in this unlikely soil. Had it been transplanted from the half-shade into a sunnier bed it might have withered as an anachronistic species. But it did very well above the greengrocer's shop, with nothing of hard-and-bright modernity to frighten away established clients.

Angela Connal sat in Henry Latham's visitor's chair and drank coffee while she chatted. It was good coffee, made from beans roasted no more than forty yards away from the front door. It was a feature of the firm—with those clients favoured enough to be offered a brew.

Latham's room was at the back of the building, so the traffic sounds were distant and even the clack of the typewriters in the general office came through only faintly.

"And so you see, Henry, I'm in a quandary." Angela put her cup down and smiled. She was dressed in a modern blouson which, though loose-fitting, was so expertly made that it enhanced the trimness of the figure.

"My dear, you've had a shock."

Henry Latham was tall—probably destined in the eyes of some people to become a dry stick of a man: a caricature of a solicitor. But at thirty-eight he was still as lithe and strong as men ten years younger. He had been a top-flight squash player in his twenties and was still hard to beat. He gave the impression of shyness, as an equal and opposite reaction to which he had developed a determination unexpected in a man so rarely called upon to show it. He addressed Angela Connal as "my dear" with an easy familiarity that natural reticence would never have allowed had there not been some deep, long-standing friendship between them. He leant over the desk to light her cigarette before continuing.

"The receipt of a letter that gives rise to doubts in a woman's mind concerning the fidelity of her husband—where previously she had harboured no doubts on that score—must shock her. It deprives her, temporarily at any rate, of her ability to think as clearly as usual. So I beg you, Angela, to consider carefully before you begin even to contemplate what I think you are hinting at—namely, divorce from James. And I should remind you, in this connection, that even proven and admitted adultery may not alone be sufficient to satisfy a court that the marriage has broken down irreparably."

She leaned forward earnestly. Latham was aware of the appeal she had for him. The voice only served to reinforce the mime. "Henry, I am positive. I haven't lost my powers of judgement. I have a feeling about this business. Call it woman's intuition if you like, but I *know* there's more to that letter . . . some deeper meaning. I really am disturbed—far more than I think I should be by the mere knowledge that James is going to bed with some other woman."

Latham got to his feet and wandered across to the window. He stood, with his back to her, looking out across the scrubby garden. She kept her eyes on him. She thought he seemed angry.

"I've never known you to make a foolish decision, Angela." His voice was not angry. He turned to face her. "And I respect your wisdom."

"How highly do you rate it?"

"Extremely high."

"Thank you. You're a great comfort, Henry. Can you now tell me what I must do?"

He came towards her, hands outstretched. "Angela, the mere thought of any man deceiving you . . ."

She smiled up at him. "Dear Henry! Help me to put right the biggest and most foolish mistake I ever made, but which you have always overlooked. The one made all those years ago when I married James."

It was enough of a promise to make his head reel, to forget the caution he would otherwise have displayed. He returned to his chair and faced her. "Let's see what we've got—apart from your feeling of unease. A typewritten letter! Anonymous! Posted in Elmhurst at lunchtime yesterday! Not much there, I'm afraid."

"And a name."

"To be sure. We can try to find Elizabeth Leacholt. It shouldn't be a difficult task." At last, a sense of caution returned. "After that, Angela, we must think again. Any future discussions must be based on what we learn in the meantime."

She smiled—a gentle smile of delight that made him want to move round the desk again to comfort and reassure her. He stayed in his seat. She said: "Henry, you're marvellous. You just dissipate difficulties, but I can't help feeling that nothing is going to be quite as simple as you are implying."

"Maybe not. But so long as you approve of what I have suggested, there is little that can go wrong at this stage. After all, we shall be taking no irrevocable action just yet."

Her eyes lit up with impish mischief. "Ah, but we are about to."

"I would strongly advise you against actually trying to institute divorce proceedings with only our present very flimsy evidence on which to base them."

She raised her eyebrows. "I'm not thinking of divorce just at the moment."

"No? That's very wise."

"But as a prelude to it, I want to change my will."

Latham was astounded. "Angela, I beg you not to do anything hastily. You could regret it if this letter turns out to be a hoax—as it well might."

There was no humour in her reply, only decision.

"I want to change my will as a precaution . . . for protection."

"As a safeguard for yourself, you mean?"

"I feel in need of one."

"Oh, come now, my dear. Safeguard? Against whom or what?"

14

"I wish I knew. It would make everything so much easier if I could identify my fears."

This time Latham did get up and come round the desk to her. He took her hands. "I didn't realise you were really frightened, Angela. How long have you had these fears?"

She looked up at him. "Ever since Robin died."

"Ah! Now I begin to understand."

He realised he had let too much of his relief creep into his tone when she replied sharply: "No, you don't. You think I'm nothing more than a neurotic woman mentally deranged by the death of her child. Admit it."

He paused before replying.

"Forgive me, Angela. I should have known better. I had no intention of treating your fears lightly. I know they must be very real to you. But look at it from my point of view—as a solicitor who is trying to think objectively. You tell me you have been aware of a vague, unidentifiable fear ever since the death of your son, four years ago. Now, just when there is a slight hint—conveyed in an anonymous letter—that you could conceivably lose the affection of your husband, these vague fears increase to the point at which you feel you need a safeguard. All that is reasonable. But judging from the steps you propose to take—namely, changing your will as a prelude to divorce—I can only assume you are hoping to provide yourself with protection at the expense of a former beneficiary."

She nodded.

"James, your husband, is your sole heir. Are you telling me that he is the source from which you anticipate the dangers you fear— whatever they are—will emanate?"

She nodded again.

"My dear, are you sure? I know James is a bit hard-headed like most clever businessmen, but he's not a dangerous maniac."

She eyed him steadily for a moment.

"You sound as if you like James. I always thought you loathed him."

"The one great thing I have against him is that you preferred him to me ten years ago. I've loved you from the first time I saw you as a teenager, and you know full well that I had hoped to marry you, but I was too damned stupid to say so before James came on the scene. Dammit, Angela, even though I was a bit backward at coming forward in those days we were all but engaged. We knew it and so did our families."

"You were always rushing off to play squash."

"I know. I've learned that no man can serve two masters—or mistresses. James came along and concentrated on you. I suppose I took you for granted. He didn't."

"No, he didn't. But apart from all that, you like him?"

"I can take him or leave him. Even his pinching you from under my nose doesn't make him a bad hat. Before your marriage you were a client of this firm, like your father. After your marriage I took on James, too. It seemed a reasonable thing to do. As I said, I find him hard-headed, but that doesn't stop me visiting you socially, or make me think he is a danger to you. If you had some factual grounds for making such an assumption, I could understand your fears much better."

She said quietly: "I have plenty of grounds, Henry."

"You have? I'd better hear them."

"Perhaps they're not factual enough for you. . . ."

"Try me."

"May I have another cigarette?"

As he lit it for her, she began to speak, quietly and without any sign of emotion. "Do you remember when Robin was taken seriously ill so suddenly? It was night-time . . ." She spoke for seven or eight minutes without interruption. Latham listened carefully to every word. When she had finished, he asked: "You've lived with this ever since?"

She nodded.

"Have you ever mentioned it to James either directly or indirectly?"

"Never directly. But you must realise it has been like a wall between us. We've not really been man and wife since that time."

Latham's thin face was serious. The jaw was set firm, and she noted that, as always when worried, he was engaged in clamping and unclamping his jaws so that the bones at the hinge were moving rhythmically in and out. She recognised the signs and so was not surprised when he said: "Thank heaven you've never actually spoken to him about it."

"Why?"

"Because you haven't a shred of evidence to prove what you think is, in fact, true. Nothing on which to base even a discussion, let alone an accusation."

"But I've just told you . . ."

"You've told me what you believe, Angela. Not evidence at all. But should your belief be right, to have mentioned it would have been dangerous. Even if it were wrong, it would have destroyed your marriage. As it is, your rejection of all marital relations may have led him to suspect that you do know what you have just told me. This, in turn, could have given rise to the personal fear that you are, yourself, now in danger. In fact, I should advise you to leave him except that your going might trigger his suspicions that you know—if they don't already exist, that is. If that were to happen—no matter where you went—your safety could not be guaranteed."

"James will never physically attack me."

"How can you be sure of that?"

"He's too clever to make any overt move that will prejudice his comfortable living and the strong chances he has of inheriting the firm, and once he knows my will has been changed, he will watch his step even more closely so as not to polish off entirely the silly goose that lays the golden eggs. It will mean that his only chance of enjoying my money is while I'm alive, because if I were to die the money would go to where he couldn't get at it. And the sooner he knows this, the easier I shall be in my mind."

"That sounds an eminently sensible view to take," agreed Latham, but not without obvious reluctance.

"It's the only way, Henry, short of leaving him. And I don't really want to physically leave my home. After all, it is mine."

"I still think—"

"No, Henry. I've thought this out. To allay his suspicions I shall tell him that my will remains changed until I am satisfied he is no longer having an affair. That will make him suppose I have acted out of pique because of the anonymous letter. But if I were to leave

17

him he would know that was too drastic a step to take on unconfirmed evidence, so he'd look for a more likely reason. That is when he'd realise that I really do know the story I've told you."

It was good enough for Latham. "In that case, and if the will is to be a simple one, I shall draft it today. Could you, perhaps, call in again at five o'clock?"

"To sign it?"

"To approve it."

"And if it is as I want it?"

"It could be signed and witnessed there and then."

"Thank you. You do see why I need it so quickly, don't you, Henry? I'll be able to tell James tonight. He'll be very angry, but at least he'll recognise that for him to try to do anything by way of retaliation would be futile."

"In that case, the sooner you tell me the dispositions you wish me to make . . ."

They spent the next twenty minutes or so discussing the provisions of the relatively simple will Angela had in mind. As he finished his notes, Latham said: "I'm going to send you off now, my dear, because I shall need all the time I've got to have this ready for you this afternoon." As he moved round to take her chair, he asked: "Why haven't you been to me to take this step before now if you have been so afraid of him?"

"Because I've never had an excuse I could use before today. The anonymous letter gives me a perfect excuse to act the part of the embittered wife. James won't like it, but it's the sort of reaction he'll understand, because it is exactly what he'd do himself if he found himself in a similar situation. Besides, perhaps I haven't really made you understand that I have never been quite so afraid of him as I have been since that letter arrived this morning. It frightened me, Henry."

"Even though James had nothing to do with it?"

"It was like receiving a sentence of doom."

He held the door open.

"So I came to you for help," she said simply.

He shut the door again. "You're not mentioning divorce to him tonight?"

"No."

"What will happen when he hears you are contemplating a petition?"

"He'll have nothing to gain by harming me once my will is changed."

"See you don't mention divorce to him, Angela. Not until we're on surer ground. Promise! For your own safety."

"I won't breathe a word, Henry. Bless you! See you at five o'clock."

They were seated at dinner. The meal was nearly over, but the conversation had been sparse. Courtesies but no pleasantries. Thank you's but no thanks. Praise for food that tasted like ashes in their mouths.

The sun, westering throughout their stay at table, had shone redly through the french window of the dining room. It was behind Angela's head, turning her hair into a halo in which individual strands took on the luminosity of floodlit shot silk. Her face, always beautiful, but not appearing quite so fine-drawn in the shadow, had an ethereal quality apparently lost on James Connal.

"You said you were going to see Latham about that stupid letter."

"There's more melon if you would like it."

"No, thank you. Did you, in fact, see him?"

"Twice. At half-past ten this morning and at five o'clock this afternoon."

"Perhaps you would now let me see the letter. Or has Latham kept it?"

"He has it."

"I'll bet he told you it wouldn't stand up in a divorce court."

"I didn't consult him about divorce. Would you like to give me a brandy with my coffee?"

He got to his feet without comment.

"I got him to draft me a new will."

"Draft?" He passed the balloon glass with its scanty contents awash in the bottom.

19

"I should have said that he completed it. I signed it during my second visit."

"Am I to be told its provisions?"

She waited until he was again sitting down with his own liqueur.

"One. Your name has been deleted."

After a moment he replied: "I see. Because you receive an anonymous letter accusing me of behaviour which I strongly deny, you cut me out of your will. Is that it?"

"What else?"

"I repeat, I deny all knowledge of this woman."

"Elizabeth Leacholt?"

"Elizabeth Leacholt or any other woman at any time since our marriage."

"I have no proof either way. When I have, I can act accordingly."

He took the liqueur at a gulp and set the glass down hard. "You have already acted. Precipitately. Jumped in with both feet, in fact."

She leaned back in her chair, one slim hand still on the edge of the table. "As a preliminary precaution."

"Precaution?" His tone was sharp. "Against what?"

She felt she had almost made the mistake Latham had warned her to avoid. But she did not rush in to retrieve it, thereby showing him she was making an effort to cover up an incautious remark. She forced herself to speak casually. "Against nothing in particular and everything in general. Perhaps I should have said precautionary measure. More coffee?"

He gestured a refusal.

"Previously I had no prepared position. Now I have one from which I can either advance or retreat as circumstances dictate."

His reply was a sneer. "Whilst admiring your tactical expertise, I can't help pointing out that to take up a belligerent posture against a non-existent threat is nothing more than shadow boxing."

"But even shadow boxing is good exercise, isn't it? Don't the professionals use it as a means of sharpening their reactions to meet whatever threats may come from whichever directions?"

Her serenity angered him. "For the umpteenth time I tell you that, as far as I'm concerned, Elizabeth Leacholt does not exist. So take up your prepared position and sign up allies like Latham if you must. But I assure you I shall give you no valid reason for declaring war."

"Until the next time."

"Oh, for God's sake, Angela, you're neurotic."

She smiled. "You must have been studying me. I ought to feel flattered. But then, psychoanalysis is your favourite hobby—after women—isn't it?"

"I'm interested—yes."

"The cause, the reaction, the result! You can rationalise all life's little problems. To what do you ascribe my—what's the term?—behavioural reactions?"

"You're as easy to read as a ha'penny book without any leaves."

"What a graphic metaphor."

"Simile."

"Never mind. Do go on. I'm interested."

"Since you insist!" He took a cigar case from his inside pocket. "Do you mind if I smoke if we're going to continue to sit here?"

"Just so long as you pass the cigarettes."

He got up and passed her the green alabaster box, an ashtray and table lighter from the sideboard. "Anything else?"

"You were going to tell me your diagnosis."

"Ah, yes." He snipped the end of the cigar. "You've been suffering from a delusion of conviction ever since Robin died." He held a match to the cigar. "You have a feeling of guilt about his death, almost as though you were responsible for it and could have prevented it."

"I wouldn't go on in that vein if I were you."

As though he hadn't heard her, he continued: "Your guilt fears have led not only to the depression for which you have to take those everlasting capsules, but also to anxiety about the guilt. In short, you have a complicated and unresolved conflict about the child—"

"Shut up, damn you! Shut up!"

"Not likely. Not now I've got started. For years you've shut out

21

reality and lived on an unrelieved diet of Valium, aspirin and warm milk.''

"Because I can't sleep. Not because oɪ guilt.''

"Rubbish! You do sleep. Every night. But you wake up early, every morning. And what's that if it isn't another sign of your anxiety depression? One which manifests itself in the usual, everlasting tension headaches.''

"You know all about it, apparently.''

"Nobody could help but know all about it after living with you in your present state. Blaming and depending! It's a well-known phenomenon.''

"I wonder why my doctor never told me this?''

"He daren't. He told me instead.''

"He told you all about me? I don't believe it.''

"Have it your way. But I'm still saying that you blame yourself for the loss of the child. And you depend heavily on me. Now—because of that stupid letter—there's a hint that you might lose me to another woman. As a result, you've become fearful of being left alone. And though there isn't a grain of truth in the allegation, you've started lashing out in a frenzy of fear—at the nearest available person. Which happens to be me. So you've cut me out of your will just to show me or pay me out in some way. That's why I say you're just too easy to read.''

By this time she had regained her composure.

"You've given me the cause of my so-called anxiety, and you've spelled out my reactions to it. What you've forgotten to tell me is what the effect will be. The final result.''

He slowly and carefully spun the cigar to remove the ash.

"Nothing. Just . . . nothing. You won't get a divorce, for two reasons. The first I've just given you. The thought of losing me after losing Robin will stop you from filing a petition when it comes to the crunch, no matter how much you threaten to do it beforehand. The second? Even if, backed up by Latham, you were to get as far as the courtroom, you would fail from lack of evidence.''

"Maybe. But I assure you that if you are keeping a mistress, I shall have the facts very soon.''

*

22

In spite of Angela's words, several weeks went by without further news of Elizabeth Leacholt, and all Latham's efforts to find her failed.

One morning in early June, another morning as lovely as only England can provide, Angela sat writing a letter at the desk in the drawing room. The front garden looked at its best. Just beyond it was the unmade-up lane that served only two houses, that belonging to the Connals and its neighbour belonging to the Brignells. Beyond the lane stretched the green belt, supposedly sacrosanct for ever and certainly unspoiled as yet.

Due to some whim of the architect responsible, the two houses had been huddled together. They were big properties, with large gardens, but between them was only the space for two garages. As she wrote, Angela could distinctly hear Mary Brignell talking to her dog. Both Zip and Mary, it appeared, were going walkies.

The drawing room door opened, and Mrs King came in. In late middle age, she was full breasted, generously proportioned and possessed of kindly features that could easily have been modelled from putty. Over her skirt and blouse she wore a modern fore-and-aft plastic cover-all gay with printed flowers.

"Oh, it's you, Kingy. Do you happen to know the date?"

"Of course I do, love. It's June 2nd. The anniversary of the coronation. Not weather like this, though, was it? They played The Queen on the wireless this morning."

"Thank you." Angela inserted the date on the letter she was writing. Mrs King still stood just inside the door.

Angela looked up. "Do you want to do this room now, Kingy? Could you be a dear and leave it for a bit? I've been meaning to write this letter for ages."

Mrs King stood her ground. "It's not the day for in here. It was something quite different I wanted to see you about."

"You sound very mysterious and . . . yes, you look quite upset. Are you in some sort of trouble?"

"Not me, love."

"When you call me love I know it's something serious and you're trying to soften the blow. You're not thinking of leaving me or anything dreadful like that, I hope?"

"As if I would, after all these years! It's just . . ." She walked towards the desk. "Well, I was upstairs, getting those suits of Mr Connal's ready to go to the cleaners and, like you said, I was making sure there was nothing left in the pockets . . ."

"And you found something valuable? Was that what you wanted to tell me?"

"I don't know about valuable, love. Mucky, I'd call it. But you'll make your own mind up about that." She put her hand in the apron pocket and brought out a photograph. "I found this in that grey check jacket."

"You sound awfully censorious. What's it a picture of?"

"Who, love. Not what. It's a photograph of a young woman without any clothes on. As I said, mucky."

Angela held out her hand. "Can I see?"

Mrs King seemed reluctant to let it go, but Angela took it firmly.

"After that letter you got . . ." began Mrs King.

"Yes, I know. But this! What would be called naughty these days, rather than pornographic or salacious, I suppose, even though the only part that's covered up is her face. I wish her hair hadn't formed a curtain like that, it covers up her more recognisable features."

Mrs King grimaced. "It's not her fizzog I'm interested in, love, nor her outsize bust and whatnot. It's the words she's written across herself at the bottom."

Angela smiled. "Rather an untutored hand. Not as mature as the rest of her seems to be. 'To Darling Jim-Jams, with love from Lea.' Quite fruity, don't you think, Kingy?"

"I don't know about fruity! If she'd had a few fig leaves it would have been a bit more decent. Anyhow, I thought you ought to see it, love, in view of that letter an' all."

"Yes. Thank you for bringing it to me. I'm sorry if you've been shocked by it."

Mrs King planted herself more firmly beside Angela. "What's she got that would shock me? It's the scandal I'm worried about."

"News of this won't get out, so why should there be a scandal?"

"Not that sort of gossipy scandal. I mean it's a scandal for girls like her to be taken in the altogether. It's boasting, that's what it is.

24

Showing off with nothing more to have a tip about than lots of girls who keep it all decently hid."

"I see. I thought you meant it was scandalous for men like my husband to be carrying such photographs about."

"That an' all. That's why I brought it down to show you."

"I'm glad you did. I'll keep it."

"Right, love. It's not as if he was a young lad who hadn't . . . Oh, never mind. I'll go and get on with my bedrooms. But if I was you, I'd talk to him about it straight. A man like him acting like that!"

"What? Oh, yes. I'll tell him he owes you an apology, too." She got up from the desk and put the photograph in her handbag. "I've just remembered, Kingy, I've got to pop out for half an hour. I'll be back before lunch."

Mrs King remained straight-faced. "Give Mr Latham my kind regards. He's a nice man, that one."

The photograph lay on the desk in front of Henry Latham. Angela was coming to the end of her account of where and how it had been discovered.

"So I brought it straight to you, Henry. I thought it might help."

"It does indeed." Latham roused himself from the "listening position" he had adopted during the recital. "My man hasn't been able to find Elizabeth Leacholt as yet—probably, he thinks, because it may not be her real name. So many young women these days call themselves models, beauty consultants and the like and adopt professional names that normal sources of information are of no help. What I mean is that Elsie Bloggs from down the road here becomes Scarlett O'Hara in the Soho strip-club where she works. However, I should think that there's a good chance that this print is traceable."

She smiled at him. "So now can I talk about divorce?"

"If you must, my dear. But I warn you, we've very little yet on which to base a suit." He spoke to her for a few minutes along these lines and ended with: "That is as far as we can possibly go at this moment. And now you must tell James that you are actively thinking of instituting proceedings."

"Must I? It sounds contrary to your former advice."

"I know. But once I start to act for you in a divorce suit, I've taken sides in law so I cannot continue to act for the other party. James will have to get some other solicitor to accept service. And to do that, he must be told what you are about."

She frowned prettily. "I've rather let you in for it, haven't I? And lost you a client."

"That doesn't matter, my dear. The important thing is, do you feel safe with him?"

"I think I do now. Changing my will made all the difference. To my feelings, I mean. Not to him. He's the same as he always was."

"Good. It's important that you should continue to live in the house and run the home."

"Aren't you forgetting? The house is mine. If anybody had to leave, it would be James."

Latham smiled. "Then don't kick him out whatever you do."

"Whyever not?"

"Because our plea will be based on adultery by James, and adultery isn't everything in divorce today. Not like it used to be. If you forced him to leave the house, he could possibly make out a case of desertion and you could find yourself what used to be called the guilty party in that respect. And in circumstances such as yours, it is not unknown for a wealthy wife to have to pay maintenance to a less wealthy husband."

"You're joking! Even to a husband who is earning what James gets as managing director of Dodson's?"

"He could, conceivably, resign and go on the dole."

She grimaced. "I wouldn't put that past him, just to spite me."

"It is extremely unlikely that he would take such a step unless he thought his position in the company to be menaced by the fact that he had been divorced by the major shareholder. But, don't forget, if it did come to a separation—that is, you and he living apart for any reason, including your kicking him out of the house—he could block your application for divorce for five years. So play it calmly, and don't condone his adultery by . . ."

"Don't make me shudder, Henry. We haven't—not for years. I'm not likely to start things up again at this juncture."

"I think I knew that. But James isn't a fool and, as I've already said, he's damned hard-headed. That, coupled with what you told me on your last visit, leads me to think that there is a distinct possibility that he might try to claim what used to be known as restitution of conjugal rights. Don't forget that once he loses you—"

He stopped in mid-sentence as she laughed aloud.

"I'm sorry, Henry, but that really is funny."

"Oh? Why?"

"Because James himself has lost no opportunity to tell me *I* daren't lose *him*. Now you talk about his difficulties if *he* loses *me*."

Latham offered her a cigarette and a light.

"James has more to lose than you. Not only your wealth, which helps to keep him in great material comfort, but also—conceivably—his job. Wouldn't the other shareholders and directors—all of them old friends of your father's—ease him out?"

"I'm certain they would. You should know. You are a share-holder yourself."

"A very minor one."

"Old Fergie would put them up to it. I have always felt the knowledge that he would fight for me to have been one of my major safeguards since Daddy died."

He gazed at her for a long moment. "I had no idea, Angela, that you have felt the need for protection for so long. You have been very foolish not to have told me before this, my dear."

"If I had come to you, you wouldn't have believed me. Not without material evidence like the letter and the photograph."

He shook his head sadly. "I still think you should have come and spoken to me about it. I'm sure that keeping it to yourself has affected your health adversely." He got to his feet. "Now, don't forget. Tell James, at the first opportunity, what you propose to do. I shall keep the photograph."

"Don't drool over it, Henry." She robbed the remark of any offence by smiling at him as she went through the door.

"Did you say you would have more mushrooms, James?"

They were again sitting at dinner. The conversation had been

27

far from sparkling, though Angela seemed to be in a gayer mood than usual.

"No, thank you." The refusal was an indication of Connal's preoccupation with matters other than food. He was a great lover of mushrooms. Usually he emptied the dish.

Angela shrugged. The gesture wasn't noticed. Her husband wasn't looking at her. As if to force him to pay her some attention, she said: "You'll find it hard to believe, in view of your recent assessment of my likely behaviour, but I saw Henry today and asked him to start divorce proceedings."

Connal was staring at her now, apparently amazed by what he had heard. "You did what?"

"I asked Henry Latham to start proceedings on my behalf. I intend to divorce you."

"And you mean to say Latham accepted? Agreed to file a suit, just like that?"

"Without a word of protest."

"Pull the other one, Angela. You've no grounds, and Latham knows it. What are you trying to do? Frighten me in some way? Because if so, you both of you should know me well enough by now to realise that I don't scare easily."

"True. We both think you'd be a pretty hard nut to crack, but Henry did seem to think that the rather fruity photograph dedicated to Darling Jim-Jams might prove helpful in more ways than one. And please close your mouth, James. If you sit there much longer with it open in mock surprise it could well stick like that. Or so my old nanny used to tell me."

"What the hell are you talking about? What photograph?"

"The coloured print of a nude. Full frontal is the modern description, I believe, though the lady in question seemed to wish to hide her facial features—probably so as not to detract from other places of interest. Did you take it yourself, James, with one of those cameras that give instant prints?"

"I still don't know what you're talking about."

"The photograph that Mrs King found in the pocket of your grey check jacket. It was very careless of you to leave it there after asking for it to be sent to the cleaners."

"I didn't leave it there. Nor did I put it there."

She put her knife and fork down very precisely before replying. "I expected you to deny all knowledge of it. To claim, in fact, that in order to implicate you in something nasty, somebody slipped it into your pocket."

"Yes. You probably."

"I also thought you might suggest that, too. But the writing on it isn't mine. And I could hardly know that the voluptuous Miss Leacholt would be known to her intimates as Lea, spelt L—E—A, could I? I should have expected Liz or Betty and not that her pet name would be the first syllable of her surname."

"To hell with it!" Connal pushed his chair away from the table and made for the door. As he reached it, he said: "This is bloody ridiculous, Angela, and you know it. I shall call on Latham to-morrow and get the whole business sorted out with him since you won't listen to sense."

"Do that. I'm sure he'd like to talk to you."

"I'll bet he can't wait. He's encouraged you to apply for this divorce so that he can have you himself. A very solicitous solicitor!"

"I was going to add that the reason he'd like to talk to you is so that he can explain in person why he can no longer keep you as a client."

Connal shut the door savagely behind him.

Latham and Connal sat opposite each other in the former's office; Latham tall and calm, Connal plump, red-faced and angry.

"So you see, James, it would be unethical for me to deal with your personal affairs any longer. I'm extremely sorry, of course . . ."

"Spare me the crocodile tears, Latham."

". . . because I don't like losing clients. Apart from that, you and I have always managed to get along tolerably well in the past, and I certainly don't like the prospect of Angela being dragged through the courts."

"Then tell me why, for heaven's sake, you've encouraged her to sue for divorce."

"I cannot discuss any aspect of the case with you. But please believe me when I tell you that I am most unhappy that relations between you and Angela should have deteriorated so much."

"You haven't any grounds for divorce."

Latham did not reply.

"An anonymous letter and a photograph I know nothing about? Come on, now, Latham. Can't you see I'm being framed?"

Still no comment from the solicitor.

"Look," said Connal angrily, "I could even accuse you of being the one who's framing me. After all, you're the man who's wanted to marry her since she was a schoolkid."

"Quite right. I have always wanted to marry Angela, but first I will assure you that I have not, as you put it, framed you, and second I will also assure you that should you suggest such a thing again I shall have no option but to enter the lists against you myself and should I need to do that believe me I shall pull no punches."

"Sorry, sorry! All I meant was that I shall contest the suit, just to make sure you don't get everything your own way, and should the solicitor who acts for me ask if I know of any man who has been a particular friend of Angela's then I would be obliged to give him your name."

"Friend, yes. Nothing more."

"Quite. One more question. What's all this about Angela cutting me out of her will?"

"Again, I am not at liberty to discuss the provisions Angela has made."

"All right. But you can at least tell me one thing. Did my wife come here to make a new will as a direct result of receiving that anonymous letter?"

Latham thought for a moment, considering whether to answer or not. At last, he said: "Yes. I think I can say that."

"You can say what?"

"That Angela came here to alter her will on the day she received the anonymous letter."

"Was it as a direct result of that letter that she altered her will?"

"As her wishes were given to me—yes."

"Thank you. That's good enough for me."

30

"I can't see what use you can make of that information. I should warn you that Angela—or anybody else for that matter—can change a will for any reason they wish, and it will still remain valid."

"I know that. But I wanted to be sure she had changed hers because she received an anonymous letter. When I find the author of that little missive I'll be able to bring home to him just what he achieved and, as a consequence, exactly what he'll have to pay for."

"You propose to institute a search for whoever wrote it?"

"Wouldn't you in my position? After all, you've been trying to find the woman who was named."

"I'll admit I don't like anonymous letters."

"That takes a bit of believing at the moment." Connal got to his feet. "I'll let you know where to send the papers of mine that you're holding. Let me have your bill."

"There will be no bill."

CHAPTER II

As HAPPENS so often in England, after its really fine start the June
weather deteriorated sadly—and with it, Angela's health. She was
one of those who are susceptible to weather. Grey days meant grey
moods. She grew more and more depressed under the leaden skies,
while a complete lack of news from Latham robbed her of what
little sleep she customarily managed to get. She had been hoping
for great things from Henry's private investigator. But though a
man of good repute, he had turned up nothing on Elizabeth
Leacholt herself, her photograph, or on Connal's association with
her.

Following Latham's instructions to the letter, Angela continued
to run the home just as she had always done. Among other things,
this included getting up in the mornings to see that her husband
was given his breakfast before leaving for the day's work.

On 21st June, Connal was to travel to Birmingham on business—a trip he took at least twice a month. The Dodson foundry
was there, as well as many small-part suppliers with whom
Dodson's dealt. Connal, a good engineer besides being a business-
man, liked to see for himself. He had decided on an early start and
had assured his wife that—in the absence of Mrs King who was on
a short holiday—he could see himself off. But despite having had a
bad night, Angela had come down with a light housecoat over her
nightdress to see that he was provided with breakfast.

The weather had taken a sudden turn for the better. Only the
afternoon before, the clouds had broken and by evening the sun
had gained the upper hand. Just as the clock in the hall struck
seven, Connal took the chain off the front door and opened it. In
the garden next door the Brignells' small dog was letting out yelps

of delight as he roamed about picking up scents and snuffing along the tracks of squirrels. Angela was just behind her husband as he turned and said: "Midsummer day, and living up to its promise for once."

"Don't grow lyrical, James. It's only seven o'clock in the morning, and it's not your style."

"I didn't ask you to get up to see me off," he said loudly. "In fact, I asked you not to. But I suppose Latham has told you not to give me grounds for any complaint that you are not fulfilling your wifely duties."

Her face was strained with tiredness. Her eyes showed her lack of sleep. She moved listlessly out on to the doorstep as if to savour the morning.

"Why don't you rest?"

"I want to fasten the door after you. Then I'm going back to bed."

"I suppose you've got the inevitable morning headache?"

"If you must know, I was dozing nicely when you disturbed me. You've been moving about the house for ages."

"It would be my fault! I'll be back by seven. Six if I'm lucky."

"There's no need to hurry. We're not going anywhere tonight."

"Not to the Wiltons? I thought we had a long-standing invitation to dinner?"

"Paula cancelled it."

"Nice of you to let me know. Did she say why?"

"Oh, for God's sake don't pretend. You know why."

"Has Charles got gout again?"

"They don't want you in their house, James. It's as simple as that."

"I don't recall my presence causing them much revulsion on our many previous visits."

She gestured wearily with one hand. "That was before . . ."

"Before what?"

"Before you started keeping a harem."

"Hell, Angela, you've not told the Wiltons all that rubbish?"

"They're my friends. I felt I had to tell somebody."

Connal's face grew red. He put his briefcase down on the step.

"Girlish confidences with Paula despite the fact I've sworn to you those allegations are untrue?"

"You've said it so often you've almost convinced me. But apart from your protesting too much, James, I mistrust propaganda. If it doesn't actively spread untruths it does nothing more than make promises which are never fulfilled."

"I don't begin to understand what all that means. What I do know, however, is that you have no proof. . . ."

"I have given my solicitor material proof of the existence of your second mistress. How many are there altogether? Hundreds?"

"Second mistress?" He sounded amazed.

"The one you are paying large sums of money to. Keeping her in some little love-nest, no doubt."

"You're raving." He picked up the briefcase and turned to leave.

"Am I? You're going now I've told you I have proof. You must have forgotten that the bank returns our cancelled cheques—at your request. A nice, straight, round-figured present of five hundred pounds to Gladys Robertson, whoever she may be."

"Gladys . . . Oh, that! Look, Angela, there's a very simple explanation. . . ."

"There always is. But this time I don't want to hear it. Listening to more of your lies would only make my headache worse."

"The everlasting excuse! Go and lie down with your pills and warm milk, Angela."

"I told you I was going back to bed."

"So you did. You won't be disturbed with Kingy away."

He turned to walk the short distance to the garage. As he did so, he could hear the sound of the chain being put on the front door and the snap of the spring lock going home. It was as he was unlocking the garage door that he heard Mary Brignell's voice close by calling her dog. "Zip! Zip! Come on, boy! Come on!" She stopped calling the dog and said "Hello, James."

"Good morning, Mary, you're up early."

"My do-gooder day. I told you last night. I'm driving the meals-on-wheels van today. But you're up bright and early yourself." She could see over the low dividing hedge quite easily, and she was standing close up to it to speak to him. "Going on the trip you mentioned at dinner last night?"

"Yes. Up to Birmingham." He swung the door up and over.

"How's Angela this morning? I didn't think she looked on top of the world at dinner."

"Mary, you're fishing. You've been out here with Zip for some minutes, so you must have seen us at the door."

She looked abashed. "Well, actually . . . Yes, I did. But I wanted to pretend I hadn't."

"Meaning, I suppose, that you overheard every word we said."

"Don't be cross, James. Zip was after something in this patch. What I mean is, I didn't come over to this side of the garden deliberately to listen. I'm sorry, James."

"Don't be. It doesn't matter. I suppose you and Michael heard all about our troubles last night."

"Oh, I heard long before that. Weeks ago in fact."

"In that case I must thank you both for still talking to me and for visiting us. Most of our so-called friends now seem to be avoiding me as pointedly as they would had I been rolling in fish manure."

"Not me, James." She laughed. "But I must say I'm a bit disappointed."

"What about, for heaven's sake?"

She laughed again. "Because, if you had to have an affair, you didn't have it with me."

"Despite what you may have been told, Mary, there hasn't been an affair. But if there ever is, I promise it will be with you."

"I'll hold you to that. Now I must fly. Come on, Zip. Time to go. Goodbye, James. Have a nice trip. Ah! There's Angela at the side door, altering the milkman's clock. Here, Zip, Zip! Come on boy!"

After she had gone, Connal entered the garage, backed out the Jaguar from beside Angela's Fiesta, and turned into the lane, heading towards the main road.

The fire engines were speeding, sirens sounding.

"Ashbury House, Fred. Hayward's Lane."

35

The driver did as instructed. He drove down Guildford Road, the broad highway to the west, announcing his urgent summons and receiving the right of way from all traffic.

Into Hayward's Lane. The heavy vehicle occupied the whole width of the lane and, despite its weight, rocked along the unmade surface as the driver sought to maintain his speed.

"How far along here, Sid?"

"If you'd use your eyes . . ."

Fred glanced up. He had been concentrating too hard on the narrow way to notice the great pall of smoke ahead. "Look at those bloody flames!"

"Christ!"

"What's up now?"

"We've come wrong, Fred."

"You said Hayward's Lane. An' we're in Hayward's Lane."

"I know that. But this isn't made up. There's no hydrants down here. All the services come from Romsey Road at the back."

"We'll reach, won't we?"

"Not bloody likely—and certainly not past that lot. You'll have to turn her, Fred."

"In this?"

"When we get to the houses."

Sid was right. There was no water supply in the front of the two houses, and to attempt to pass the burning house or its neighbour carrying heavy equipment would have risked lives and wasted more time than turning the equipment and making the way back to Romsey Road.

Four—perhaps five—minutes were wasted.

The vehicle braked and came to rest where the backs of the grounds of the two houses touched Romsey Road. As the siren died, the firemen started their hurried drill of dismounting, opening lockers, unreeling hoses and locating hydrants.

Sid took charge.

"Hoses, lads. Don't bother about foam for this lot. It's like a blow-torch. Worse than the blitz."

Fred said: "It's too far gone. We'll never do anything with that. Not if we had half a dozen appliances."

"We can try. Mr Cranby can call out more if he wants to."

"Not worth it. It's burning from ground to roof. See! There's a stack going already."

Fred's prediction was true. A crash of falling masonry: the roar of the flames: the babble of onlookers: the noise of the firemen running hoses into the long garden.

Fred said: "Here's Cranby now."

A small car drew up in front of the engine. Sid said to the newly arrived officer: "I've told the lads to concentrate on the garage, the trees, and the house next door."

"Reckon you're right, Sid. Never seen anything like that lot. You'd think it was made of matchboard. OK. I'll report in."

The sub-officer used the radio in his car. "Hello, Control. Arrived here eleven thirty-three. Large house. Complete combustion. Reckon we can isolate but not extinguish with what we've got."

The unseen voice acknowledged receipt and then asked: "Do you need more help?"

"Hardly seems worth it. The whole house has gone up. We can't save it, but as it's completely detached we can, as I said, stop it from spreading with what we've got."

The control voice spoke again. "Have police reported on situation regarding inmates?"

"Not yet. We're at the back in Romsey Road. The address was properly given as Hayward's Lane, but there aren't any hydrants there. I reckon the police will be round at the front. Not that it'll be any good because I can promise you there's nobody left alive in that little lot—if there was anybody in there, that is."

Sid joined him. "I've told the lads to keep well away. There's been some falling already."

Cranby sucked his teeth. "Any sign of anybody in there?"

"Not as we've seen. And even if there was . . ." Sid shrugged as the best way to finish the expression of his opinion.

"What d'you really reckon, Sid? I don't like it myself. You got here, in what? Fourteen or fifteen minutes?"

"We went to Hayward's Lane and had to come back. I'd say about seventeen, myself."

37

"Yes . . . Well, it's gone up like a bloody atom bomb in that time and that's not right."

Sid shook his head. "Oh, there's been funny business, if you ask me. Plain as the nose on your face it wasn't some smouldering fag-end that sent that lot up." He turned to look down the road as a police siren sounded and a patrol car turned into the road and drove at speed towards the gathering crowd of onlookers.

"Somebody's in a hurry. Looks like Sergeant Saunders. He'll want to know what we think about it. Right nosey, that one."

Saunders was heavily built, but he quickly covered the ground between the patrol car and the two men standing by the engine.

"Glad you're here, Mr Cranby. There could be a woman in there."

"What?"

"If she was in there, she'll be a goner by now," said Sid lugubriously.

"Name of Connal," said Saunders.

Cranby said: "Hang on, Sergeant. Could be, you said. How do you know? Anybody see her at a window? I want to be sure, because I'm not risking my lads' lives trying to get into that lot if she isn't there."

"Nobody's seen her. But her car's in the garage and we know she never reckons to go out without it. She wouldn't, would she, not from Hayward's Lane?"

"What do the neighbours say?"

"There's nobody in next door. I've been told the man, Mr Brignell, is at work and his missus is away for most of the day doing meals on wheels."

Cranby leaned into his car and picked up the microphone. "Hello, Control. Police say there could be a woman in Ashbury House. I want at least one more appliance and a turntable, smartish."

"Understood, out."

Cranby turned to Sid. "Get them playing on the back of the house. First floor windows. All hoses."

Saunders said: "I'll just move this crowd back and make a few more enquiries round about. I'll keep in touch. I reckon you'll have

38

to think how you'll get a turntable near. You'll have to take the fence down to get it in."

Cranby grunted, then said: "Before you go, Sergeant . . ."

"What's up?"

"You didn't ask me how I think it started."

"I never do. Who can tell from out here?"

"Look at it."

"How d'you mean, look at it . . . ah! You reckon there's been a bit of hanky panky?"

"That lot didn't go up on its own. Not that fast, it didn't. It was helped."

"You're saying it was started deliberately?" Saunders had forgotten the crowd and was taking out his notebook.

"That's what I think. Ask me how in a few hours from now—when it's cool enough to inspect what's left."

Saunders put his book away. "Right. I'll do that. But you know what you're saying, don't you? If some fire-raiser did that and there's a dead woman inside, it's murder."

Some five hours later, shortly after half-past four in the afternoon, Sergeant Saunders, accompanied by Detective Inspector Hill of the Elmhurst C.I.D., picked his way across the still steaming debris of what had been Ashbury House.

Cranby saw them coming and made his way towards them. Saunders said: "When he heard what you told me this morning, the D.I. decided he'd better come along himself."

"And I've got C.F.O. Mailer with me for the same reason. He's still ferreting round but he wants to see you—and the D.I., I should think. It's as I expected. There's a lot about this he doesn't like."

Hill said quietly: "Nor me, Mr Cranby. We've established there's little doubt Mrs Connal was inside. Apart from her car still being in the garage, her neighbour, Mrs Mary Brignell, has now returned. She said she overheard Mrs Connal say early this morning that she was going back to bed after seeing her husband off to work. Evidently she had a headache she was going to try to sleep off. The husband, James Connal, confirms it."

"You've managed to get hold of him then? The last I heard was he'd gone away for the day."

"He'd gone to Birmingham. He's back now. We managed to get a message to him at his foundry."

"Isn't he some big bug in Dodson's Engineering?"

"Only managing director. His story is that he set off soon after seven this morning hoping to get to the M1 before the worst of the traffic built up."

"Leaving his wife to go back to bed?"

"She got up to see him off. She had a dressing gown on over her nightwear because as soon as he'd gone she was going to take something for her head and then go straight back to bed."

"Sounds as if she was there all right. Probably too dopy to know the place was on fire. Overcome before she could wake up, perhaps. We'll look for her when we can. And here's the boss coming."

C.F.O. Mailer was picking his way across the debris. The others moved to meet him.

"What have you got to tell us, Mr Mailer?" Hill asked.

Mailer was tall and thin and as sad-looking as an aging labrador. He grimaced as he spoke. "It was arson all right. Started in three places—p'raps simultaneously—among highly inflammable material."

"How do you know that?"

"Hot spots are as easy to find as kiss your hand. There's three of 'em. All sites of original fires. I didn't know the lay-out of the house, but according to the woman next door it was the same as hers, but a mirror image. She let me in to check."

"Check what?"

Mailer turned and pointed a long, bony, grimy finger. "You'll see that east wall's mostly standing because the internal part of the stacks acts as a buttress. I went up there earlier to have a look. . . ."

"How did you manage that?"

"I kept the turntable back a bit—just until it was cool enough to swing me over that way."

"I see."

"And I saw, too. I saw the fire had been started on three levels."

"Three? It only had ground and first floors, didn't it?"

40

"That's right. But if you have a look at the lay-out next door you'll be able to pinpoint the sites. The ground floor outbreak was in the cupboard under the stairs. The first floor one was in an airing cupboard on the landing, and the third was in the loft."

"Somebody had gone into the loft to start a fire?"

"A sort of luggage room in the false roof. Yes, all the marks are there on the brickwork of the stacks."

Hill looked grim. "And you reckon all three went up together?"

"I'm pretty sure."

"The one under the stairs didn't set light to the others? I mean, there'd likely be loads of highly inflammable stuff in an airing cupboard and luggage room, and I've heard tell these fires can simply gallop up a stairway."

Mailer nodded. "That's so. But I'd say not in this case."

"How can you tell?" asked Saunders.

"The sites weren't directly above one another. Flames and fire leap upwards. Oh, I know they creep sideways, but that needs time. And there wasn't any time-lag here. From the time the alarm call was phoned through by a Mr Parker—a milkman— to the arrival of our first appliance was roughly a quarter of an hour."

"Roughly?" asked Hill.

"My chaps got here quick enough," said Cranby. "But they'd been given wrong instructions. When Parker, the milkman, rang in, he correctly said the building on fire was Ashbury House in Hayward's Lane. But when the equipment got there they found the lane was not made up and so there were no hydrants. They wasted five minutes in reversing the engine and coming back to Romsey Road to connect up."

"So they first saw the fire after twelve minutes."

"That's right. It was so bad even by then they wondered whether it was worth trying to save."

"That's right," said Mailer. "In those twelve minutes the whole house was alight from top to bottom. Complete combustion."

"That's so," said Saunders. "I was here myself just after the engine. I made the same mistake. I went to the front, seeing the address was in the Lane, so I can vouch that the front was a goner before I arrived and by the time I got round to the back, the walls were caving in."

"And how!" said Cranby.

Mailer nodded. "So you see, Mr Hill, it couldn't have happened with just one fire starting up in a small way at just one point. And it wouldn't have burned that fiercely if the fires hadn't been helped with a supply of inflammable material that would get them blazing—not just smouldering—in a big way right from the start."

Hill offered cigarettes. When they were alight, he said: "Three fires going up simultaneously would mean some accurate timing device was used. Electrical, I suppose?"

"Bound to be. It's easy enough these days, with timer-plugs as common as makes no matter. A house like this would likely have two or three they could pre-set to bring the lights on if the house was left unattended. Then there are all the cookers with clocks to start them up at pre-set times."

"They'll have survived, won't they?" asked Hill. "They're not made of inflammable material."

"Mostly plastic, and that melts."

"We could still see what time they were set at, perhaps."

Mailer shook his head glumly. "No use. You could set them ahead of time or behind time." Seeing Hill looking mystified, he asked: "Have you got central heating, by any chance?"

"Yes."

"It switches itself off overnight?"

"Yes."

"At what time?"

"Half-past twelve—till six-thirty in the morning."

"What happens when you change to summer time or winter time or there's a power cut?"

"I have to alter the clock."

"What to?"

"To agree with the correct time."

"Say you didn't. What then?"

Hill nodded. "I see what you mean. It would read as though it would go off and on at the right time, but because the master clock would be wrong, the schedule would be shot to pieces."

"Right. In other words, you can do what the hell you like about timings if you put the timer-clock wrong. So even if we find any of them, we can't trust them to tell us the truth."

Again Hill nodded. "Say they were used—what would it be for exactly?"

Mailer looked glummer than ever. "I can't tell you that yet, either—if I ever can."

"Guess."

"I reckon it would be to complete a circuit in which there would be a series of electric elements—like bar fires."

"Go on."

"If I'm right, it would mean there was something highly inflammable in contact with the elements so that when they started to glow they'd go up in flames."

Hill shook his head. "I don't reckon so—not just that."

Mailer looked hard at him.

"I've tried burning things in my garden," said Hill. "Things like blankets and sheets in an airing cupboard are bloody hard to send up straightaway. What I mean is, they'll burn all right, but this chap must have wanted to be sure he got an immediate blaze. He could do it with a few bits of scrumpled-up paper perhaps, but he couldn't be certain they would set fire to folded sheets and suchlike. And he had to be sure, didn't he? He couldn't have afforded for anybody to notice the smoke from just one smouldering fire."

"I see what you mean. But I can tell you this. He didn't use paraffin or petrol."

"No?"

"I've sniffed around and there's no sign."

Hill asked: "Could you really smell paraffin after a blaze as fierce as that?"

"Yes. It permeates brickwork and debris and the oily fumes hang about. And there are no signs of an explosion, either."

"So that rules out the possibility of a gas escape."

"Right. I'll be putting it all in my report."

Hill didn't want to let him go. "What about my point? About the difficulties of being certain you can get a fire going quickly? Whoever did this had to be sure."

Mailer nodded. "You're right, but we can only speculate. There was no petrol or paraffin used."

"You're saying it was something that doesn't leave traces like paraffin?"

"Something that leaves no trace at all. That'll stump you, won't it? Not being able to pin it down, I mean."

Hill scratched one ear. "What about Mrs Connal?"

"All you'll see of her will be a few charred bones in a heap of twisted bed metal. If you're lucky, one of the bits will have a wedding ring on, which her husband might recognise."

"I've asked Connal about identifiable items—apart from teeth. She didn't wear a locket or permanent earrings, but besides her wedding ring she always wore an eternity ring with rubies and diamonds set alternately round it."

Cranby, who sounded as if he felt he was being left too much out of the conversation, said: "That'll be a help. Gold and precious stones don't usually come to any harm in a fire."

Mailer ignored the information. "If they're here, we'll find them when everything is properly cold. Probably quite quickly if we look immediately beneath where her bed was." He started to move off, obviously intent on leaving them, but again Hill stopped him.

"Can we talk about doors now?"

"I thought you'd want to get round to those. I've collected all the bits and pieces in one spot over here."

As they picked their way across the rubble, Hill asked: "You've concentrated on the doors?"

"I knew you'd ask questions about them."

"I suppose all the woodwork's gone?"

"All of it. Three doors. Back, front and side. But the door furniture, being metal, is still more or less as it was."

They reached a clear area where a piece of hardboard had been laid on the ground to take whatever items were retrieved from the ruins. Mailer stooped and picked up three fire-stained spring locks. "Yales," he said. "All in the locked position. You can see their tongues are protruding. Here, catch hold. They're quite cool now, so you can handle them."

Hill took them, more for appearance's sake than for any other

44

reason. He could see what Mailer had said was true. Then he asked: "Just because all three doors were locked doesn't mean that an intruder couldn't have been inside, does it?"

"At the time of the fire, you mean?"

"Before. He could have let a door lock automatically behind him when he left."

"He could. But look at these chains." Again Mailer stooped and this time came up with three dusty red items. "They're distorted and almost welded into the slides. But they were all on."

Hill said slowly: "That's conclusive enough."

"Nobody can put a chain up after he's left a house."

"Unless he got out through a window."

"There's that."

"But those chains leave us with several interesting possibilities."

"Do they? I'd have said they narrowed the field a lot."

"In one way, perhaps. But her husband says Mrs Connal was a neurotic woman. And neurotic women sometimes do bloody stupid things like locking themselves inside a house and then setting fire to it."

"Committed suicide, you mean? It's a hell of a way to do away with yourself even if you are neurotic. I've never met up with it in over thirty years of dealing with fires."

Hill felt the need to pacify the lugubrious fire chief. "She could have done it accidentally," he suggested.

"She couldn't, you know."

Hill sighed inwardly. "I'm not forgetting what you've said, but if a time-plug was used, it could have been put in a circuit somebody knew she was in the habit of using regularly."

Mailer said: "I don't reckon anything about this job was left to chance. If you go to the trouble of laying three fires to make sure you get a fast burn, you don't mess about with off-chances. Besides, for Mrs Connal to switch on, she'd have to be up and about, which means she might have escaped."

"Thanks. So that line of thought is ruled out. Now, there could have been two people in the house."

Mailer was apparently not keen on such flights of fancy. He

45

looked at Hill pityingly for a moment and then asked: "Is that just speculation or is it based on some fact you've got hold of?"

"One of the possibilities, that's all. I've got to consider them one by one."

Mailer conceded the point. "If you're right," he said slowly, "it would mean that the fire-raiser murdered Mrs Connal and then committed suicide in a bloody ghastly way."

"He needn't necessarily have murdered her first, but stranger things have happened."

"OK. So I'm to look for two bodies." Mailer sounded resigned. "But I still reckon the pyromaniac left the house before Mrs Connal locked up and went back to bed."

"Meaning her husband murdered her."

"It's not my job to say so."

"But you've got your reasons."

"To arrange three sites for simultaneous combustion would take a bit of time besides having a knowledge of the lay-out of the house. I can't see how any outsider could move about inside a house for any length of time without being heard or seen."

"Good point," said Hill. "That about being seen or heard, I mean. And as it follows that whoever laid electric cable and planted material in those three cupboards had to have a good idea of the lay-out of the house, well . . . it's the knowledge only a husband would have, normally."

"To say nothing of having to have a working knowledge of electrics. That's a man's job. If not an electrician's somebody who knows . . ."

"The husband is a working engineer."

"So I've heard."

Sergeant Saunders said: "There's also the point that whoever did it knew that the housekeeper was away and Mrs Connal would be alone."

Hill gave him a nod of approbation for this contribution before turning back to Mailer. "If we add all this to the undisputed fact that most murders are committed by members of the victim's family, it begins to look as though we shall have to put Mr James Connal through the hoop."

46

"And you won't like that, I suppose," said Mailer, "Connal being a wealthy and important man."

"I don't care who he is," said Hill decisively.

"Well, it's for you to decide. When we've finished our inspection I'll let you have a full report."

"Thanks. I hope it will have a few hard facts in it to bolster up all the circumstantial evidence."

Mailer didn't like the implication any more than Hill had enjoyed the hint that questioning the wealthy Connal would be distasteful.

"To hear you talk," said the C.F.O., "anybody would think you'd got problems ahead."

"If you find the remains of a body in there, I will have."

"I reckon you've got the husband halfway to the dock already. I'll bet a quid you'll have Connal in front of the magistrates inside a week and in front of a judge and jury inside three months."

CHAPTER III

MAILER WOULD HAVE lost his bet, but only because of the vagaries of the Law Term sittings. The earliest date on which the administrator of the circuit could bring Connal before judge and jury was the first week in October—the first week of the Michaelmas sittings. Murder, under its designation of an upper band offence, must by law be tried before a High Court judge—preferably one of the two presiding judges of the circuit which normally covers the area in which the alleged crime has been committed.

So Connal appeared in Elmhurst Crown Court on the first Wednesday in October, charged with the wilful murder of his wife, Angela Connal. Mailer's estimate had been exceeded by one month—probably because the C.F.O. was ignorant of the minutiae of the legal system. D.I. Hill did not demand the quid staked by the fire chief. He was satisfied enough with getting Connal into the dock.

Satisfied, that is, until fairly late on the Friday afternoon. Then his feelings underwent a change.

Sir Francis March was appearing for the Crown and Mr Mark Cudlip was leading for the defence, before Mr Justice Cleghorn. The jury had four women members.

Hill had assessed all twelve of the jury as being—in his view—sentimental, by which he meant that they would be duly horrified at the thought of a man burning alive his beautiful wife, and so would have little hesitation in finding such a man guilty of murder.

The prosecution had presented a case which relied largely on circumstantial evidence—though none the worse for that. Particularly when tendered so skilfully by Sir Francis who was justifiably regarded as a master of the epigram because he was

48

usually able to round off every examination with so telling a piece of phraseology that even the most prosaic of evidence lingered in the mind.

So Hill had been satisfied until the afternoon of Friday, when the lowering autumn sunshine began to gleam irritatingly through the south-western facing windows of the courtroom.

The defence had called William Parker, the milk roundsman who delivered daily to Ashbury House and who had raised the alarm on the day of the fire. Hill had been unable to decide quite why Parker had been called, unless it was merely to prove what was not in question—that Ashbury House had, to all outward appearances, been as normal as it had been on every previous day—until the fire had taken hold, that is. Sir Francis, who before the trial had not thought the milkman's evidence of sufficient importance to have him called as a prosecution witness, now seemed to be highly pleased that the defence had seen fit to call him.

Hill, seeing Sir Francis' air of satisfaction, listened extremely carefully as Mr Cudlip examined Parker. When defence counsel sat down, the D.I. was still convinced that the roundsman's presence in court was of no value to either side and was not going to make a scrap of difference to the outcome of the trial.

Hill noted that Sir Francis glanced at the courtroom clock as he rose to cross-examine.

"Mr Parker, you told us that you left three pints of milk at the side door of Ashbury House on the morning of the fire."

"That's right."

"Why the side door?"

"Why the side. . . ? Oh, I see. Why don't I go to the back door, you mean?"

"Precisely."

"Well, two reasons, really."

"What are they?"

"First, for those two houses in Hayward's Lane, I have to go in from Romsey Road. And they are long gardens. If I had to walk down one and out and then down the other and out, it would take me a month of Sundays. So I had an agreement with Mrs Connal and Mrs Brignell. Their side doors are opposite each other and very close. But the back doors are a long way apart."

"The houses are mirror images of each other?"

"If that means they're the same but the other way on, yes."

"Please continue."

"The two ladies let me deliver at the side doors and they left a little gap in the hedge behind the garages so I could get through. That way, I only had to walk down and up the gardens once."

"An amicable arrangement, in fact?"

"I'd have had to stop delivering, else. Not worth the time and sweat to go that far twice. And it would have been worse delivering from the Lane, because they were the only two houses down there. It would have taken half an hour that way."

"I understand. You said there were two reasons for using the side door. What was the second reason?"

"The side doors are nearer the kitchens than the back doors. Cock-eyed planning if you ask me. Whoever designed—"

"Thank you, Mr Parker. At what time did you call at Ashbury House on the morning of the fire?"

"Near enough ten o'clock. I said that before. I said the round's pretty regular as to time."

"Are you an observant man, Mr Parker?"

"My wife says I'm not. She says I can't see things in front of my nose."

"Do you agree with your wife?"

"In some ways, but not when I'm doing my round. It's my job, see. And I know everything and everybody round there. I reckon that if there was anything wrong I'd spot it quicker than most."

Hill began to wonder what Sir Francis was getting at and also how long the judge would allow such apparently fruitless questioning to continue. Probably old Cleghorn had so much respect for prosecuting counsel that he assumed Sir Francis had good reason for the line he was taking with Parker. If so, Hill thought, the judge was mistaken.

Sir Francis agreed amiably with Parker. "I'm sure no one in this court would dispute your claim. After all, we have heard that you were the first to realise Ashbury House was on fire. You were the one who acted promptly and called the fire brigade."

"That's right."

"The defence called you as a witness primarily to hear that you—a very observant man—noticed nothing out of the ordinary about Ashbury House when you delivered milk there at ten o'clock that morning."

"There was nothing wrong."

"Just an ordinary day, in fact?"

"Yes."

"Mr Parker, earlier we heard from Mrs Brignell, a neighbour, that she saw Mrs Connal at the side door altering the milkman's clock. That was at the time Mr Connal left the house that morning."

"Maybe. I wouldn't know about that."

"Would you know if Mrs Connal is in the habit of setting your clock herself?"

"'Course not. She had her housekeeper who did that. Mrs King."

"Quite. Now, Mr Parker, you have not been in court to hear what previous witnesses have said. But Mrs Brignell has assured us that she also saw Mrs Connal set your clock the previous evening when she put out the milk bottles."

"Most likely, I'd say. Folks usually do that sort of thing the night before."

"Mrs Brignell said—almost in passing—that Mrs Connal set her clock—and here I quote—for 'two pints as usual'. Yet a few moments ago you stated that you left three pints of milk that morning."

"I did. I suppose that's why Mrs Connal altered it. She wanted three."

"We'll accept that explanation, Mr Parker. But Mrs King, who was not at Ashbury House that day, but who has, nevertheless, appeared as a witness in this case, has stated that two pints was the usual amount. Yet you left three pints—an unusual amount."

"Yes."

"And in spite of this you say there was nothing unusual about your call at Ashbury House at ten o'clock that morning?"

"Oh, I see. I didn't know . . . I thought you meant about the house and grounds, like."

"I meant everything, Mr Parker. So now, will you tell us what you did find on your first visit that morning?"

"I knew they wouldn't be having a party that night, like."

"Really? How did you know? Did somebody tell you?"

"No. The cream indicator said they didn't want any cream. They always ordered cream when they were having a party."

"Anything else?"

"Nothing, except as I've said I was asked to leave the three pints which I'd never done before when they weren't having a party. Two as regular as clockwork. There's only the three of them in the house."

"So there was an anomaly there. No cream, no Mrs King, no party, yet three pints of milk. How do you explain this?"

"I don't have to. People can order as much as they like when they like. And often do."

At last the judge intervened.

"Sir Francis, where is this line of questioning leading us? Is the amount of milk that was delivered important to your case?"

"Not fundamentally, m'lud. But, because Mr Parker is a defence witness, I wished to show the court that the Crown views him as being in no way hostile to the prosecution, and to emphasise to a somewhat greater degree than my learned opponent has seen fit to attempt, that this witness is a highly observant and reliable witness as to fact."

"Please take it from me, Sir Francis, that the court is satisfied that the witness is an observant man. I fail to see how establishing this assessment of Mr Parker's various abilities will help the Crown at this stage."

"M'lud, the prosecution had intended to call this witness for the Crown, but . . ."

"The defence nipped in before you, is that it?"

"Exactly m'lud."

"Such a confession of ineptitude on the part of the prosecution still does not explain why you are taking so much trouble with Mr Parker. If I did not know you extremely well, Sir Francis, I should be inclined to think that you were playing for time. In case I am mistaken and you *are* wasting the court's time, let me remind you that this witness is the last on the defence list, and I need hardly point out to you that by now your case has been put to the court almost in its entirety."

"Exactly, m'lud. I wished to establish Mr Parker's reliability before questioning him on certain important points yet to come."

"For any good reason, Sir Francis?"

"Certainly, m'lud. I consider that the replies I get from Mr Parker will provide me with a basis for cross-examination of the accused should he enter the witness box. My learned colleague has not yet informed me whether he intends to call his client, but I wish to be prepared should he do so after Mr Parker leaves the box."

"I see. But please, Sir Francis, get to whatever point it is you wish to make."

"As m'lud pleases." March turned to face Parker. "Apart from the mystery of the milk, everything else about the house was normal."

"It was at ten o'clock, but it wasn't just after eleven o'clock."

"Tell the court what happened then."

"By soon after eleven o'clock I was coming back up the other side of Romsey Road, delivering, when I seen the house was on fire."

"And what did you do about it?"

"Ran into the next of my houses, asked to use the phone and dialled 999."

"Highly commendable. When you first saw it, was it a big fire?"

"Not really."

"Would you please tell us exactly what you saw?"

"It was funny, really. I can remember looking straight at the back of Ashbury House—among the trees, like—when I got off the float. I was facing that way when I got down, you see, and I was right opposite. But I didn't see any flames at all."

"What did you see to alert you?"

"Smoke. Coming out of the roof tiles. Funny effect, it was."

"Enough smoke to suggest to you that something was wrong?"

"That's right. I ran to the gate so's I could see more of the house.

53

There was smoke coming out of the windows."

"Which ones? Ground floor? Bedrooms?"

"It was the roof, mainly. Anyhow, that's where I could see it most—up against the sky. But it was coming out at all levels, but not from all the windows if you get my meaning."

"I think the jury will realise what you mean. You saw smoke coming from at least one window on each floor. What then?"

"Well, by the time I'd made the 999 call and come outside again to the float, there was flames. Big ones. Mostly at the top, but they was soon all over."

"Soon? How soon?"

"I wouldn't put it at more'n a minute, but it was probably two. Before I could open the gate and get down the garden, anyway."

"Have you ever witnessed a fire before? In real life, I mean. Not on television or films?"

"Often enough. I'm nearly sixty. I was in the war."

"Have you ever seen one that behaved like the one at Ashbury House?"

"Definitely not. Except when a petrol dump brewed up in Normandy."

"So it was not what you would call a normal fire?"

"If they was all like that, you could demob the fire brigade. They'd be useless."

"Quite. You say you went into the garden to see what you could do to help?"

"That was the idea. No go, though."

"But you were looking hard at the house all the time?"

"Looking to see if there was anybody at the windows."

"You were concentrating on the windows, but to the best of your knowledge, was there any person—perhaps a stranger—acting suspiciously in or around the Ashbury House property?"

"Not that I saw, sir. Not then or at any time I was in Romsey Road. And I keep my eyes open, like I told you. But of course, I only saw the back of the house."

"Thank you, Mr Parker. I have no more questions."

Cudlip half rose from his seat to say he had no intention of questioning the milkman further. The judge thanked Parker and graciously gave him permission to leave the witness box.

D.I. Hill was still unable to see why Sir Francis had examined Parker so closely. All that rubbish about having wanted the milkman as a Crown witness! And what was the outcome? He had succeeded in emphasising that even to the lay mind the fire had been no ordinary one; but this had only backed up Mailer's expert testimony on exactly the same point. The court, Hill was sure, had already—before Parker's appearance—accepted that the fire was arson: a deliberate and successful attempt to destroy Ashbury House and—or so he believed—its occupant.

Hill's opinion of Sir Francis sank sadly. He believed that until the beginning of the cross-examination of Parker, the Crown had been doing nicely, had been ahead on points. Now, he thought, the jury had become a little restive, bemused, perhaps, as to why the milkman had been kept so long in the box merely to substantiate facts which were already known and accepted.

"Mr Cudlip, does the defence intend to call any more witnesses?"

"I call the accused, m'lud. James Laurence Connal."

Connal was still sleek and well-covered, despite more than three months in custody. No doubt he had made full use of those privileges allowed to as yet unconvicted prisoners who are prepared to pay for them. His pale grey suit was newly valeted. His gingery hair was carefully tended. His brown shoes shone as he was escorted from the dock to the witness box.

". . . the whole truth and nothing but the truth."

Connal had elected to give evidence on oath.

Hill settled himself to pay close attention. This appearance should be the highlight of a trial which, though superficially exciting, had so far been mundane and had not gained great attention in the press. Cudlip was a mild-mannered man. He had conducted the defence quietly, producing no startling shocks, no sparkling cross-examination. It only remained to be seen how he would use the personality of the accused in his own defence.

Sir Francis had made a point of stressing to Hill, after the court had risen the previous afternoon, that Connal was out of the common run of people who found themselves in the dock on such a charge. Sir Francis had given it as his opinion—after studying his demeanour in the dock—that Connal was the type of man who could well make a good impression when speaking on his own behalf. Hill, who had interviewed Connal several times at great length, agreed. He also added that in his opinion, Connal was a plausible bastard. Sir Francis, who had been looking for pointers as to the best way in which to deflate Connal when the time came, had thanked Hill for the impression, but asked for more specific help. Hill had been unable to oblige. Now Connal was in the dock, and apparently as calm as a sleeping babe.

Cudlip started off.

"You are James Laurence Connal, husband of the late Angela Connal with whom you resided, until the time of her death last June, at Ashbury House, Elmhurst?"

"I am."

"How old are you?"

"Almost forty."

"What was your occupation at the time of your arrest?"

"I was managing director of Dodson's Engineering, and had been for almost the past seven years."

"So you assumed the responsibility for an important firm at the age of thirty-three. Were you not a little young to hold such a position?"

"I don't think so. There are many senior directors younger than that these days, and I think our balance sheets show that the firm prospered under my direction."

"Was there, however, in your case, an element of nepotism in the appointment?"

The judge intervened to explain to the jury what nepotism meant.

"Yes, of course there was. I married the owner's daughter. But I must say in fairness to myself that not only do I possess a first class engineering degree and a diploma in management studies to fit me academically for the post I held but, before I married—and by that I mean before my wife and I were even aware of each other's existence—I had worked my way up the hierarchy of the firm to an associate directorship while I was still in my twenties. After I became a director I was entertained, at his home, by Mr Dodson, who at that time held both the chairmanship and the managing directorship. It was then that I first met his daughter."

Cudlip had waited patiently for his client to finish this lengthy reply, obviously confident that it was making a good impression on the jury. But he sought to reinforce the effect.

"So though your position may have been due to the fact that you were the son-in-law of the founder of Dodson's Engineering, you could be confident of earning a good living on your own merits, had you never met your wife?"

"I was doing so before I met her."

"Thank you. I wished to make that point quite clear to the jury as I may wish to return to it later and as, no doubt, my learned opponent will wish to touch upon it also."

The judge intervened. "Pray leave crystal-gazing to the astrologers, Mr Cudlip. And leave Sir Francis' future actions where they should rightly be—in the future."

"As you wish m'lud." Cudlip turned back to the dock. "Mr Connal, I should like you to tell the court, in your own words, what your relationship with your wife was up to the time of her death. Were you happily married?"

"Exceedingly so for some years."

"Then the atmosphere changed?"

The judge again saw fit to intervene. "Mr Cudlip, you have asked the accused to inform the court on this point in his own words. Now you proceed to lead him. One or the other, Mr Cudlip. Which is it to be?"

"I'm sorry, m'lud. I would like the accused to use his own words."

"In that case, kindly instruct him to continue."

Cudlip said quietly: "You were saying you were exceedingly happy for some years after your marriage."

Connal spoke up clearly, with just the right touch of sorrow and regret in his tone. "For more than five years, actually. After two and a half years of marriage, our son, Robin, was born and we were—well, just a very happy little family. It was about the time

57

that Robin was born that my father-in-law relinquished the managing directorship and I was appointed to succeed him. He retained the chairmanship. He was a widower, and my wife was his only child. At his request we went to live with him at Ashbury House. He was doing considerably less than formerly at the factory, and he seemed completely wrapped up in his little grandson. That was why he wished us to share his home. He lived for just another thirty months and then died, with little warning. It was a tremendous blow to my wife—naturally enough. But we had our son and each other and she was well on the way to being her old self again when a far greater tragedy hit us."

Cudlip said courteously: "Pause for a moment if you wish to, Mr Connal."

"No, thank you. I'll carry on."

"I, however, would like a moment," said the judge, without looking up from his writing. It was some seconds before he asked: "When you say your wife was well on the way to being her old self again, are you suggesting that the death of her father affected Mrs Connal more severely than one would expect a grown-up, married woman to be affected by such an event?"

Connal appeared to think briefly and then replied: "Until that time, m'lud, I had always considered my wife to be a very stable woman. I expected the death of her father to grieve her deeply, because they had always been very close. But I did not expect that she would be so completely bowled over for so long. Her nervous prostration lasted for several months."

"Thank you. Please proceed, Mr Cudlip."

Cudlip turned to Connal. "You mentioned a greater tragedy. . . ."

"When Robin was just three, he was suddenly taken ill—at about ten o'clock one night. He had had one of the immunisations that children have these days. The doctor came at once and confirmed what we could see for ourselves—that the child was in great distress. The doctor assured us, however, that the prognosis was good and . . ."

"One moment, please." The judge turned to the jury. "The word prognosis, for those of you unfamiliar with it, simply means the doctor's forecast of the probable course a disease is expected to take. A good prognosis, therefore, means, in this case, that the doctor fully expected the child to recover promptly." Having cleared up this point, the judge nodded to Cudlip.

"Carry on, please, Mr Connal."

"Because the prognosis was good, the doctor considered it would be unwise to move the boy to hospital during the crisis. And, he told us, once the crisis was over there would be no need for hospital treatment. So Robin stayed at home. My wife refused help in nursing him . . ."

"Why?" asked the judge.

"I can't say exactly why, m'lud, but it seemed to me that as a direct result of her nervous trouble after the death of her father she became very possessive over our son. It was as though she had lost one of her props when Mr Dodson died, and she intended to cling to those she had left—our son and myself—at all cost."

"Thank you. Please continue."

"As I said, Angela refused help in nursing Robin, and she carried on all through that night and the next day. She insisted that I should go to work during the day as our woman help would be about the house until I got back from the office to be with her. I suppose she thought I would be more of a hindrance than a help."

"I must interrupt you again, Mr Connal."

"M'lud?"

"If you had a woman help in the house, could she not have helped with nursing the boy?"

"Our help was Mrs King who has already appeared as a witness, m'lud. Both of us trusted Mrs King completely, but when it came to nursing Robin even a tried and trusted friend, like Mrs King, was not allowed to take direct care of the boy during his illness."

"You are saying that your wife had an obsession?"

"Or a phobia, m'lud."

The judge peered over his glasses. "Are you sure you have chosen that word correctly?"

"As colloquially used, m'lud, yes."

"Ah!" The judge turned to the jury. "Strictly speaking a phobia

59

is a lasting abnormal fear or great dislike of something. In this connection I would like you to disregard all idea of fear and to accept that the accused meant that his wife had a great dislike of entrusting her little boy to another's hands. You may assume that such an attitude was unreasonable. If so, it follows that you must accept that Mrs Connal was not quite herself at the time."

Cudlip rose to murmur his thanks to the judge and to ask Connal to continue.

"Very late that second night, Robin seemed to be breathing more steadily. The doctor came and was so satisfied with the child's progress that we all thought the worst was over. After the doctor left, I managed to persuade my wife to get some rest. She slept in a chair from sheer exhaustion and relief. But the chair was in the boy's room. She would not go to bed. While she slept, the child died in his sleep. I was watching him myself, but I was unaware of the fact that as he grew more peaceful, his breathing was growing weaker. It was the most terrible misjudgement on my part . . . but . . . but everybody who has seen a child slumber knows that normally there is hardly a stir . . . no movement. By the time I began to suspect that all was not well, it was too late."

"Take a moment to compose yourself, Mr Connal."

"I apologise, m'lud. But every time I recall that night . . ."

"Quite, Mr Connal." The judge wrote for a few moments and then turned to Cudlip. "We will proceed when the defence is ready to do so."

Cudlip asked Connal. "What effect did this tragedy have on your wife?"

"The worst possible, I'm sorry to say. You see, she blamed herself—utterly. Quite why, I never understood, but partly, at least, I think the reason was because she had been asleep at the time."

"Only partly?"

"And partly because had she agreed to engage a nurse, she would not have exhausted herself to the point where she just had to sleep. It was a cause of bitter regret to her. And coupled with this was the feeling that she might have done something actively to save him: that she, who knew him so well, would have realised that he was growing weaker—where I did not—and so could have taken some steps to save his life."

Cudlip intervened. "Are you suggesting that your wife suffered from a guilt complex from the time of your son's death?"

"It was diagnosed as guilt depression and anxiety. They manifested themselves in several ways from then until the time of her own death."

The judge coughed and looked up. "Diagnosed by whom?"

"By Dr Aileen Hamnett, m'lud. Dr Hamnett was the consultant psychiatrist at the Elmhurst Hospital."

"Was?"

Cudlip came in. "Dr Hamnett was killed in a car accident eighteen months ago, m'lud."

"Do you not intend to substantiate the accused's assertion by calling a competent medical witness?"

"The defence has tried to find an expert witness, m'lud, but has failed. Mrs Connal was a private patient of Dr Hamnett and no other psychiatrist was involved."

"I have no wish to further hamper the defence, Mr Cudlip, but you will appreciate that when the time comes it will be my duty to point out to the jury that you are producing unsubstantiated testimony."

"I understand perfectly, m'lud, but we are content that the court should be given my client's version and that the jury should —after your Lordship's instructions to the members—be free to make their own assessment of the validity or otherwise of the testimony they hear."

"Very well."

"Thank you, m'lud." Cudlip said to Connal, "You had just told the court that your wife's guilt depression and anxiety manifested themselves in several ways. Please tell us what these manifestations were."

"My wife became a poor sleeper. I don't mean that she became a chronic insomniac. But despite any form of sleeping pill or tranquilliser—such as you have heard our family doctor describe in his evidence—she would only sleep for a comparatively short time each night. She would then wake very early and just lie there, thinking about heaven knows what, but invariably giving herself headaches."

"Can you describe these headaches?"

"They were, I believe, the customary tension headaches."

"You believe?" demanded the judge.

"I am reporting what the psychiatrist said, m'lud."

"You mean what the doctor told you about your wife's condition?"

"Yes, m'lud."

The judge said to Sir Francis: "Do you have any objection to the accused putting to the jury as reported fact what his wife's doctor told him of her condition?"

"No, m'lud. Subject to the usual provisos, we have no desire to hamper the defence."

"Good. Please continue, Mr Cudlip."

Asked to do so by his counsel, Connal began speaking again.

"The psychiatrist who treated my wife told me that a recurrent morning headache is a common enough phenomenon. In most patients, however, they occur at about eleven o'clock each day—for some reason totally unknown. Angela was an exception. With her they occurred much earlier in the day as regular as clockwork in frequency, but varying slightly in timing. Usually they came on between seven and eight in the morning. Very often she would get up and would then have to return to bed with a glass of warm milk and a pill. She always knew when she had to take these measures, and so did I."

"When?"

"If the slightest thing happened to upset her, m'lud. I had to tread on eggs before leaving for work each day."

"Thank you."

"Were there any other manifestations of her condition?" asked Cudlip.

"One major one. After Robin's death she would never again consent to our living as man and wife. Angela steadfastly refused to return to normal married life."

"Did you try to persuade her to do so?"

62

"Of course. I felt that if we could have had another child, its presence would have lifted her out of her depression. But her only reaction to my suggestion was one of revulsion."

"So for over four years you cherished and cared for a wife without conjugal reward?"

"I—we—were getting along very well. It was a slow business, but I had great hopes that before very long . . . Well, my wife was a most attractive woman and I loved her. For several months I thought there were a few hopeful signs, then . . ."

"Then what, Mr Connal?"

"That anonymous letter arrived."

"The one which informed your wife of your liaison with a certain Miss—or was it Mrs?—Elizabeth Leacholt? The one the prosecution has already exhibited?"

"Yes."

"Are you saying there was no foundation for that letter?"

"Rephrase," ordered the judge before Sir Francis had time to object.

"Was there any foundation in truth in the contents of the letter?"

"None whatever. I never knew such a person as Elizabeth Leacholt ever existed—or even if she does exist at all."

"You doubt her existence?"

"If she were ever on it, she seems to have disappeared off the face of the earth."

"Certainly we have heard that the police have been unable to trace her and also that a private enquiry agent employed by your wife's solicitor, Mr Latham, was equally unsuccessful. Is that why you doubt her existence?"

"For those reasons and because I—the one who was supposedly having an affair with her—knew that the affair itself was a figment of someone's imagination. So if the affair was non-existent, why not the other supposed party to it?"

"I take that to be a rhetorical question, Mr Cudlip?"

"Quite, m'lud. It was the question posed by the accused to himself when trying to account . . ."

"Yes, yes. Please go on, Mr Cudlip."

"If I had been having a clandestine affair—with Miss Leacholt or any other woman—it should have been easy enough to bring to light," said Connal. "What I mean is, that she and I would, of necessity, have had to live within striking distance of each other, I would have thought. After all, when I was not in the office I was very rarely out of my wife's company, and she knew it."

"Have you any idea—any idea at all—who could have written that letter to your wife?"

"None. It was typewritten, so I couldn't recognise the handwriting. And there was no signature, as you know."

"Yet your wife appeared to believe it, despite your protestations of innocence?"

"I put her attitude down to her neurosis. Had she been her normal self, she would have laughed it away."

"I see. We will leave that point there and return to the letter itself. The police have admitted in evidence that they have failed to trace the typewriter on which the letter was produced. To your knowledge, did any of your acquaintances possess typewriters?"

"Just about all of them, I think. At one time, personal possession of a machine—whether one ever used it or not—was considered to be one of the status symbols. Loads of people have them tucked away."

"I see. I would now like to turn to the photograph that has been exhibited in court. What I believe is nowadays known as a girlie picture was found in the inside pocket of one of your jackets by Mrs King who alleged that she discovered it there when getting some of your garments ready to go to the cleaners. It was addressed 'To Darling Jim-Jams, with love from Lea'."

"I never saw it. My wife gave it to her solicitor before I had a chance to look at it."

"The prosecution wishes the jury to believe that because your name is James, the endearment 'Jim-Jams' could refer to you."

"Is that a question, Mr Cudlip?" asked the judge.

"If not exactly phrased as a question, m'lud, it was nevertheless expected to evoke a reply."

"I see. Your client is supposed to divine your intentions?"

"No, m'lud. I will put the question direct."

64

"Thank you."

"Does the pet name 'Jim-Jams' refer to you, Mr Connal?"

"I cannot recall anybody ever addressing me in that fashion. Jim, sometimes, perhaps, but mostly James."

"Thank you. The prosecution has also sought to make capital out of what they claim is a strange double coincidence. The signature on the photograph is Lea, spelt L—E—A. A slightly unusual way of spelling the more common L—double-E. They suggest that as these are the first three letters of the surname of the mysterious Miss Leacholt, they are a pet name for that lady. Here, they say, is something which demands explanation. A photograph addressed to a person who could well be you from a person who could well be the woman with whom your name had been linked previously. They reinforce their argument with the fact that the picture was found in your pocket. What explanation can you give to enlighten the prosecution?"

"I can't attempt any explanation. I have, as you can imagine, cudgelled my brains to arrive at some theory as to how the photograph got into my pocket. I certainly did not put it there."

"Can you suggest who did?"

"No. And from what I heard earlier, neither can the prosecution."

"They suggest you did. But the photograph was allegedly found by your housekeeper, Mrs King. Do you have any reason to doubt her word?"

"None. I have known Mrs King for many years now, and have never had cause to doubt her integrity. I would go further, and describe her as unflinchingly truthful and trustworthy. If Mrs King says the photograph was in my pocket, that was where it came from."

"Did you suspect your wife of putting it in your pocket?"

"When she first told me about it—and I was very angry—I did actually accuse her of doing so. But I admit I was wrong. It was an outburst in the heat of the moment. I felt . . ."

"Yes?"

"I felt I was being shot at, but I didn't know who was doing it, or from which direction the bullets were coming. All I knew for certain was that I had never seen the print."

"Did you tell your wife you had never set eyes on it?"

"Of course. But I couldn't convince her. I've already explained why."

"Have you?" queried the judge. "Ah! You are implying that your wife had set up some mental barrier between you. Is that it?"

"Yes, m'lud. And yet. . . . Although I hadn't actually changed her mind about the divorce she had set in motion after the appearance of that photograph, I think I had achieved some success in that direction until she discovered the cheque I had written for Miss Gladys Robertson."

"Tell the court about it, please."

"Miss Robertson had been a schoolmistress. She retired from teaching at the age of sixty but decided, for financial reasons but chiefly because she was still very active, that she could not stop work altogether. For some years, as you may know, typists and clerical assistants have been difficult to get, so when Miss Robertson applied for a very general sort of clerical post at our Birmingham foundry, we were glad to take her on. Her work was excellent. It was a revelation to us all. She was a born administrator. Within a very short time she had pulled the general office round into very good shape by introducing new systems and so on."

"Is all this really necessary, Mr Cudlip?"

"We think so, m'lud. Vitally necessary."

"Oh, very well."

Cudlip nodded to Connal to continue.

"We very soon decided that Miss Robertson was worth more salary than we had at first offered her. But she refused to accept more because it affected the income from her pension and she was adamant that we should not simply replace money which she considered hers already by right and contribution. She worked for us for five years only. Unfortunately, a stint of five years at her age does not bring anybody within the scope of superannuation schemes. Miss Robertson therefore did not qualify for a pension from us. To show our appreciation, however, we had intended to make her a lump sum award as a retiring present. But even this would have been heavily taxed and she wouldn't have that at any price. The only possible way to implement our ideas was for me to make her a gift out of my own pocket. I wrote her a personal cheque for five hundred pounds. The gesture was by no means as generous as it may sound because, as you can guess, as managing director it would be possible for me to recover the money in some way."

The judge looked over his spectacles. "Are you suggesting that you would have defrauded the Inland Revenue?"

"Avoidance of tax, m'lud. Not evasion. There are fringe benefits which are perfectly legal perquisites."

"I see. Is your company particularly free with such benefits?"

"I made sure it was not, m'lud. My wife was the major share-holder. I had no desire to see the value of her holding diminished by a give-away policy of fringe benefits."

"But you proposed to reimburse yourself?"

"Justifiably, m'lud. I had paid out five hundred pounds on behalf of the company. I was entitled to get it back, tax free."

"And Miss Robertson?"

"A personal gift is not taxable, m'lud."

"It was not a personal gift if you intended to reimburse your-self."

"If you say so, m'lud."

"I do say so. However—" he addressed the jury, "—the defendant is not being tried for tax evasion. I merely wished you to realise that his apparent magnanimity was based in illegality, no matter how much or how little you admire his gesture in supplying Miss Robertson with a tax-free gratuity."

Connal continued.

"We still had our cheques returned by the bank after cancel-lation. My wife used to look through them to compare them with the statements. She spotted the payment to Miss Robertson. I hadn't mentioned the matter to Angela, and she jumped to the wrong conclusion."

"And what was that wrong conclusion?"

"That Gladys Robertson was a woman I was keeping some-where for my own pleasure."

"But surely Mrs Connal could have been convinced that such a state of affairs was not true?"

"She didn't mention it until I was literally outside the house on the morning of the fire. She presented her knowledge as the final straw and though I tried to explain, she accused me of lying. The doorstep did not seem to be the right place for an angry exchange, and I was in a hurry to get to Birmingham, so . . ."

"So? Mr Connal."

"I left without clearing the matter up."

"Did this cheque destroy what little success you might previously have made towards convincing your wife that the woman Leacholt did not exist?"

"Though Angela insisted that the cheque gave her material proof that I was—as she put it—keeping a harem, I had every reason to believe that I could sort the matter out when I returned home."

"Your neighbour, Mrs Brignell, has told the court that she overheard this last conversation with your wife. Was her evidence correct in substance?"

"As far as I can remember, it was. The account was, I should say, correct in every significant word. But, of course, Mrs Brignell did not know the background to the conversation, and without that knowledge the incident would tend to show that I am a great womaniser. The prosecution has attempted to interpret it that way."

"And you claim you are not a womaniser?"

"I do. Neither the police nor Latham's private investigators have been able to show that I am. Nor will they. But yet it was on this account that my wife had instituted divorce proceedings."

"And also on this account, Mr Connal, that you stand accused of murdering your wife. Did you in fact do so?"

"No."

"Did you in any way scheme or conspire to bring about your wife's death?"

"No."

"Do you profit in any material way from your wife's death?"

"No. My wife had cut me out of her will as a preliminary to divorce. The house was hers, too. I have simply lost my private possessions which, though covered by insurance, have not been replaced by the insurance company because they will not pay an owner who is accused—as I am—of destroying his own property."

"You did not set fire to your property?"

"No."

"Expert witnesses state that your house was destroyed because three serious and simultaneous fires were started or were caused to start by a human hand. Was that hand yours?"

"No."

"Expert witnesses also testify that the doors of the house were locked and chained so that nobody could have entered or left without your wife's knowledge. Can you account for this?"

"It was usual for my wife to chain the doors when she went to bed, if there was nobody besides herself in the house. As I have said, she was a nervous woman in a state of great anxiety. So the fact that the doors were found to have been secure does not surprise me. But if I might make a suggestion . . ."

"Please do."

"Could an intruder not have entered by a window? Daylight break-ins are not unknown, and from what I have heard about the severity of the fire, I should be surprised if all the windows were later found intact."

The judge said: "Thank you. The prosecution witnesses have admitted that they are not certain such a break-in did not occur. But you may be sure the possibility is one I shall put to the jury later. Please carry on, Mr Cudlip."

"Mr Connal," said Cudlip quietly, "could your wife have taken her own life?"

"I would prefer not to think so, but . . ."

"Carry on."

"But she was a neurotic of some years' standing and, because of our misunderstanding that last morning, she was very over-wrought . . . I just don't know . . . if . . . could she have. . . ?" Connal shook his head in bewilderment.

"Thank you, Mr Connal. That is all I wish to ask you, but now, no doubt, counsel for the prosecution will wish to ask you some questions."

"You are indulging your hobby of prognostication again, Mr

Cudlip," said the judge. "Sir Francis, is your cross-examination of the accused likely to be protracted?"

"I have several points I would like to put to him, m'lud."

"An hour?"

"That would seem to be a fair estimate, m'lud."

"Very well. As it is now almost six o'clock, and as if to give the lie to Mr Cudlip's clairvoyance, have you any objection to postponing your examination of the accused until Monday morning? Before you reply, please take into consideration the fact that the accused has already spent two arduous hours in the box and so has, I suggest, some claim to a period of rest."

"I have no objection whatsoever, m'lud."

"Thank you, Sir Francis. The court will adjourn until Monday morning."

CHAPTER IV

THERE WERE TWO courts in the Elmhurst court building, one on either side of a vast first-floor foyer, approached by a flight of wide stone stairs that led up from the entrance hall below, turning back on itself halfway to form the stairwell that separated the courtrooms. The foyer was stone-flagged and provided with wooden benches around the walls. There were two meagre radiators which could never have hoped to raise the air temperature even if the foyer had been enclosed. With the stairway acting as a huge wind tunnel the place, in winter, could profitably have been hired out as deep-freeze storage. Here, each morning, when courts were in session, sixty or seventy jurors sowed the seeds of pneumonia while waiting to be called or dismissed. Witnesses shivered with cold or nervous fatigue, sometimes for hours on end. Elderly court ushers in vergers' gowns shambled to and fro about their business, the purpose of which was rarely apparent. Bewigged juniors strolled in pairs, hands in pockets, to show off their finery to any who might care to notice it and to suggest that they were there, ready to do instant wordy battle to earn the few paltry guineas with which their skilled advocacy was so meagrely rewarded.

Hill was passing through this gloomy hangar on the Friday evening when he heard his name called.

"Inspector Hill!"

March was standing, still gowned, at the door of counsels' robing room.

"Sir Francis?"

They met halfway. "I was hoping I would catch you. He's going to get away with it, you know."

"I'm afraid so, sir. I thought we were well ahead on points until he got into the box. Then . . . well, that cheque of his! You could see the jury sympathised. You could see them churning it over—a man being pilloried for making a kindly gesture, etcetera. Even the judge's remarks about tax evasion brought them down on his side. They can't wait to let him go, and he's as glib as hell."

"More important, Mr Hill, he's guilty of premeditated murder."

"You're satisfied he is, sir?"

"Never more sure of anything in my life. In my business—as in every other—one develops a professional nose for things that smell. Connal is a rogue, of that I'm sure. He's a rogue actor and he's won over his audience."

"You've still got to cross-examine."

"I told you at the outset that I'd nothing concrete to pin on him."

"I know, sir. I wish I could help."

Sir Francis still used a silver cigarette case. He produced it now from his waistcoat pocket and offered it to Hill. As they lit up, the barrister drew Hill over towards the large windows to get a little more privacy.

"I asked you for ammunition, simply to make it easier all round to get the conviction. You couldn't produce it. No! I'm not blaming you. It just wasn't to be had. But it is a habit of mine, when I'm prosecuting, to watch the demeanour of the accused in the dock pretty closely. I find I get to know them that way. Remember, the first I see of them is when they appear in court, so I have no opportunity of getting to know what I'm up against before a trial begins."

Hill nodded. "I hadn't thought of it like that, sir. Defence counsel can have as many consultations as he wants and can get to know his man thoroughly."

"Just so. I study my subject and try to fathom him—what manner of man he is, what he's thinking, what his reactions are to what witnesses say and so on. It helps. Not always, but often enough."

"You've watched Connal throughout the trial?"

"I have. I came to the conclusion that though he was a bit big-headed, which is a dangerous trait in a criminal entering the witness box, he was nevertheless going to be a hard nut to crack. I guessed that he would have some sort of hypnotic quality—rhetorically speaking."

"And now you've heard him you know you were right?"

"I get no pleasure from it, believe me, because as well as knowing I'm right, I know he's guilty."

"His attitude shouts it aloud," grumbled Hill.

"To you and me, but not to the jury. However, there was something else. Some fact that came out in court today, but eluded me."

"That's unusual, I'd have said, Sir Francis."

"Without wishing to sound too bumptious, I agree with you, Mr Hill. And that makes me think that it was not some legal titbit that jogged my old brain, otherwise I'd have snapped it up—because it would have been right up my alley, so to speak."

"Meaning it was something more in my line, sir?"

"I think so, but the hell of it is, I can't give you a pointer. Your own antennae didn't start quivering at any time, did they?"

"No, sir, more's the pity. I'd like to see Connal go down. Not just because it's my case, either. I honestly believe he's guilty of a calculated murder—a really clever one. And I don't want clever murderers at large on my patch."

"Trouble is," grumbled March, "he's scotched the obvious motive. He made a point of stressing that he won't gain financially and I can't rebut that. But there must be a motive. Must be."

"It'll be one of the usual. Lust, greed, jealousy, hatred and so on. But he's shot them all down, sir. Spiked your guns before you've fired a shot, you might say."

Sir Francis looked around for an ashtray, failed to find one, and ground his cigarette butt underfoot. "Would you say he's a vain man, Mr Hill?"

"And how! Completely in love with himself, sir."

March said quietly: "In love with himself? You know, Mr Hill, I think you've put your finger right on it."

"I have, sir?"

"My namesake—another Francis—Bacon, not March . . ."

"I've heard of him, sir."

73

"I'm sure you have. He wrote a bit about subjects that modern authors would shy away from. Of Vain-Glory, True Greatness, Wisdom and like subjects. One of his works, 'Of Wisdom for a Man's Self', had a passage apposite to this case."

"Oh, yes, sir?"

"I must see if I can get it right. Let me see now . . . 'It is the nature of extreme self-lovers, as they will set a house on fire, and it were but to roast their eggs.'"

Hill stared at him for a moment before commenting: "You know, Sir Francis, I wish I'd heard that before this case came to court. I reckon it would have helped me to appreciate more what I was up against in tackling Connal. It could have made a difference."

They stood in silence for a moment, looking out at the darkening sky. Hill appeared a little indecisive, as though there was something he wished to say but didn't know quite how best to phrase it. At last he chose the direct way. "We've got very little time left, Sir Francis. Is there anything I can do?"

March turned to him. "Would you mind if I were to make a suggestion which, on the face of it, may look as if I doubt your professional ability? Needless to say, I don't."

"Go ahead, sir."

"Thank you. We've only got a weekend break in which to come up with the answer. We've got that because I angled for it deliberately. I prolonged the examination of that milk-roundsman in order to make sure that the trial would not end this afternoon.

Hill sighed with relief. "I was wondering what you were up to, sir."

"Thought I was maundering, eh? Well, I wasn't. I'd come to the conclusion we've already discussed concerning Connal—so you see it was before he appeared in the box—and I started to play for time in the only way open to me."

"Now we've got a breathing space, sir, what do you suggest we do with it?"

"It could prove to be a godsend if we could get another opinion on our material. What I mean is, a fresh mind might be able to find the chink in Connal's story that I have missed but which, if found,

74

might be of use to you and, consequently, to me."

"I'm with you, sir."

"But because time is short, it has to be a highly trained mind."

"What sort of highly trained? Legal?"

"A policeman's."

"Keep going, sir," said Hill heavily.

"Who taught you your stuff?" asked March with a smile.

"Superintendent Masters of the Yard, sir. I was his sergeant for long enough."

"Good, is he?"

"The best there is. But we'd never get him."

"We could try—if you wouldn't object."

"Object to George Masters? Me? I'd be as pleased to see him as . . . Well, he can come here any time he likes as far as I'm concerned."

"Fine. George and his wife are by way of being friends of mine. So if both of us ask for his help, we'll get it. Oh, and by the way, he's Chief Super now. They've shoved him up another rung on the climb to the Commissioner's chair."

"I should hope so," said Hill. "But I'll have to tell my boss."

"Will he mind? I know he didn't call in the Yard, and rightly so, because you have dealt with this one very ably. But as you yourself have agreed, the personality of the accused has become a factor of more importance than either of us could have guessed. We've been outwitted by the unusual. To beat Connal we shall have to take a few unusual steps. Will your Chief Super agree to that, do you think?"

"Even if he doesn't, Sir Francis, he'll do as you ask. As far as he's concerned, anybody representing the D.P.P. is God Almighty. He's a good copper, but he gets a bit overawed."

"Can I leave it to you to let him know—as a courtesy? I'll ring Masters."

"If he agrees to come, sir, what would you ask Chief Superintendent Masters to do?"

"To help us—you and me. All I propose—with your permission, and as a favour to us—is to ask him, unofficially, to read the documents in the case to see if he can spot the point I missed—or any other lead for that matter. Would that offend you?"

"Offend me? Not likely. But just as a matter of interest, Sir Francis, we are in the Metropolitan Police area here, you know. Right on the fringes, but the Division is part of the Met., so there should be no inter-force bother."

"Excellent. Can I leave it to you to get an up-to-date transcript of the proceedings so far? I'll ring Masters and ask him to come to my hotel. Can you be there by eight-thirty?"

Hill nodded. "Your room?"

"Yes. A hundred and eighteen. It's a suite. I've got a sitting room attached, with a table and a few chairs in it. We can talk there."

"Come along. Let's get out of here before the phone rings again."

Chief Superintendent George Masters took his Aquascutum from the coat stand and slung it over his arm. Detective Chief Inspector Green ground out the end of his cigarette in the ashtray and got to his feet. He was already wearing a heavy, dark coat, having called in at Masters' office preparatory to leaving the Yard. They were to go together. Green's wife, Doris, was at Masters' small house behind Westminster Hospital. She was there for the ceremony of bathing the baby. This took place daily at half-past five so that the child—Masters' five-month-old son— could be snugged down and asleep by six. Doris Green was a devoted assistant at these ablutions. She adored the child as much as she and her husband adored Wanda, Masters' wife. This evening, the D.C.I. and his wife were to baby-sit for the Masters' who were—for the first time since the birth of young Michael—to go out to dinner.

Masters held the door open to let Green precede him. But that was as far as they got. The phone rang.

"I'll answer it," said Green. "Pretend you've gone."

Less than twenty seconds later he was holding out the handset to Masters. "Sir Francis March. He wants to talk to you."

Masters listened for more than a minute.

"I understand, Frank. You and Hill are both asking that I should come to Elmhurst. You I could refuse, but not Hill. When he left us, both Bill Green and I promised him help at any time should he need it. Bill is with me now. He'll want to give Hill a hand, too. No, no trouble about our coming. Elmhurst is in our bailiwick and we're free of major entanglements at the moment."

Green grimaced the question "When?" He got his answer from Masters' next reply.

"No. Not tonight, Frank. First thing tomorrow morning. We're both busy tonight. Yes, engagements we can't break. Sorry."

A moment later Masters put the phone down. "Scarper, Bill. I shall be late as it is."

They walked the short distance to the little house that Masters had been lucky enough to find a couple of years earlier. Minute, tucked away up a cul-de-sac, it was too small for a family home, and the Chief Superintendent would probably have to start looking for something bigger. But Green referred to it as Wanda's Palace, which gave some idea of how he regarded the result of the couple's tireless efforts to perfect the cottage. To let it go would be a wrench, but Masters had hardened his heart: he wanted space and a garden for young Michael, and Green could do nothing but agree.

During the walk Masters told Green what he had learned from March.

"You mean to say that because he's losing a case he wants to call us in?"

"On a voluntary, consultant basis."

"It's a new one on me."

"And me. But you'll come, won't you?"

"I'd like to see what sort of a fist young Hill is making on his own."

"Humbug," retorted Masters. "You've been keeping a surreptitious eye on his major cases ever since he left us."

"First-hand, I mean," replied Green, unabashed. "He's good, but he hasn't enough drive. Lacks a bit of tenacity, I reckon. It'll do him good to have a refresher course from us."

"We're only going there to read the court proceedings."

"And I don't think! I'll bet you we'll get involved."

"We can't. The accused is in the box. His own counsel has let

77

him have his say and now all that remains is Sir Frank's cross-examination. No more witnesses, nothing."

"Ah, well! But I still think March wouldn't have asked us to go if he didn't think we could do something."

"Rotten chairs, these, Frank," said Masters. "Ribbed velveteen upholstery and no room for the posterior."

"Sorry George," replied March. "Will you have some refreshment? Coffee or a drink?"

Masters, dressed in a grey Windsor check suit, seemed larger than ever when sitting in the puny chairs left over from the post-war austerity period. Across the table from him, Green was still reading documents. He was a page or two behind Masters. Hill was doing little except act as a go-between, passing the papers between his two former colleagues and occasionally answering the odd question.

"Best keep a clear head so early in the morning," replied Masters, "so make it coffee, Frank."

While Sir Francis ordered coffee, Green tossed the last of the papers on to the table.

"Finished?" asked Masters.

"I can understand what young Hill meant when he said it was a bit of a bastard. The Lord Harry only knows what he expects us to do with it."

"Are we beaten before we begin?" asked March.

"Time," grunted Green. "And it's not only new evidence we've got to get, but facts that are admissible at the fag-end of a trial. You'll not be able to fling in just any old thing, will you? The judge and defence counsel will see to that."

Before Sir Francis could reply, Masters said: "Before we get too downhearted let us give thanks for the unwritten law which says that the accused, when testifying in his own defence in a murder trial, shall not be interrupted, challenged, curtailed or in any other way prevented—by prosecuting counsel, that is—from convicting himself out of his own mouth."

"Connal didn't convict himself," said Hill glumly. "If you'd been there, Chief, you'd have seen the jury just lapping it all up. No wonder Mr Cudlip let him run on virtually without interruption. He saved his own neck, figuratively speaking, and he certainly got away with murder—literally. I wondered why you didn't rise to object at times, Sir Francis."

"I must admit I was sorely tempted," said March. "But there were two reasons why I held my tongue. The first you know about. I wanted him to stay in the box prating away for as long as possible."

"If you'd interrupted it could have prolonged his stay in the box."

"Not necessarily. If the judge had upheld me it could have meant that a lot of what he said would have been left unsaid. But that is by the way. The second is the reason the Chief Superintendent has touched on. Neither Mr Justice Cleghorn, nor any other judge for that matter, would ever interfere with the testimony of a man giving evidence on his own behalf when on trial for his life. The unwritten law that George mentioned is that the judiciary should never appear to interfere with a man's right to say what he wants to say in defence of his own neck."

"And that applies to counsel?"

"To Crown counsel. The defence counsel has always been at liberty to curb or direct in the accused's best interests."

Hill said: "But nobody's neck is at risk these days."

"Agreed. But the habit has continued in murder trials, even though life is not at stake."

Masters, who was tamping Warlock Flake into a large-bowled cadger's pipe with the slim fingers that seemed so out of place on such a huge man, came into the conversation to say: "Don't run away with the idea that the habit grew out of pure judicial or advocative charity."

"No, Chief?"

"The appearance of the accused in the dock is a relatively recent phenomenon. Until very shortly before the First War, an accused man was not allowed to utter a word in court. But when this custom was changed, prosecuting lawyers realised that if they gave the accused enough rope he would, ninety-nine times out of a hundred, hang himself. You see, most murderers were either poor speakers, or else they were big-headed show-offs, guaranteed to say more than was good for the health—literally."

Green asked: "Why in hell's name didn't defence counsel stop 'em?"

"They did, whenever possible," said Sir Francis. "And that gives the lie to George's uncharitable remarks about lawyers."

Hill tapped the transcript of the trial on the table in front of him. "Mr Cudlip let Connal go on unchecked."

"And you know why," said Sir Francis. "Connal is the Chief Super's one hundredth man. The one who gets away with it. Connal is obviously a practised speaker. Cuddles Cudlip knew his client would drag in a lot of extraneous stuff that would help his case and to which I—under the gentleman's agreement—wouldn't object. For instance, there was the business about the cheque. It had nothing to do with the charge so you didn't investigate it thoroughly and I didn't intend to mention it."

"If I'd investigated it and you'd then examined me about it," said Hill, "what good would it have done us?"

"None. But you saw how it affected the jury in his favour."

Hill grimaced and turned to Green. "Glib as hell, he was. His insincerity made me squirm in my seat, but the jury swallowed it whole."

Surprisingly, Green replied: "Don't forget that you and Sir Frank have had quite a bit of experience at summing up criminals and weighing the value of evidence. Those poor so-and-so's on the jury haven't. They don't like being there, either. They get corns on their backsides from the pews in the box, and so any little ray of sunshine that comes to brighten up the session as they sit there, cooped up and longing for a fag or wanting a pee, is going to be like a breath of fresh air from the slums. Of course they're going to lap it up."

Hill stared at him, open-mouthed.

"I'm right, matey. That's why they don't see Connal as glib and plausible."

"I'd have thought, if they were so uncomfortable in the box, they'd have been cynical about every word they heard."

"Maybe," replied Green, offering a crumpled packet of

Kensitas. "But not when it's somebody as clever as your Mr Connal, able to batter their ears with as big a load of hogwash as he put across. It was a fairy story for them. He didn't miss a trick."

Hill nodded to show he appreciated the point. Sir Francis said: "You're right, Mr Green. He modestly admitted nepotism, bravely stated how much he trusted the housekeeper, shame-facedly confessed to wrongly accusing his wife and described how he had done good by stealth. Sheer empathy—all of it. They were all putting themselves in his place and thinking they'd all have done exactly what he was describing in similar circumstances. Look how hesitantly he suggested a break-in and wept tears over the death of his son which he blamed—by implication—on his wife. And how delicately he led them to perceive how he had suffered and been deprived because of her mental illness. And there was more than just a veiled suggestion that the same mental illness had driven Mrs Connal to take her own life. What a performance! Mark Antony couldn't have done it better. No wonder Cuddles Cudlip gave him a free rein."

"Have you finished, Frank?" asked Masters. "We've got a job to do and not much time in which to do it."

"I haven't finished—not by a long chalk. I could go on for hours. But I'll stop if you've found something that strikes you as offering us a lead."

"He must have done," said Hill, "otherwise he wouldn't have said we should thank our lucky stars for that unwritten law."

Masters was about to reply, when Sir Francis again intervened. "All I want, George, is one dirty great devastating question with which to rock Connal back on his heels on Monday morning."

Masters said, a little impatiently, "If you'll keep quiet for a minute or two, Frank, you may even get it."

"And that," said Green, "means we'll be working all weekend, for a bet."

"Maybe," said Masters. "One blessing is that as the trial is being held in Elmhurst, all the witnesses should be close at hand."

"I'll willingly work all night if it means we'll nail him," grunted Hill.

"Except for meal-breaks," said Sir Francis. "Lunch in about half an hour."

"That should just give me time to put forward my hypothesis," said Masters.

"Only a hypothesis, Chief?" Hill sounded disappointed.

"Sorry. We've only got time to work on assumptions. Routine is out. I must assume, for the purposes of this exercise, that Connal is guilty. Because you and Sir Francis say so and not because the D.C.I. and I have proved him so to our own satisfaction. So everything we do from now on must be based on that assumption, and being so based, must be a hypothesis."

March said: "Not to worry, Mr Hill. Surely a hypothesis from George Masters is good enough for us."

Masters allowed this compliment to go unremarked. He looked across at Green. "Let's look at Connal's evidence first. You said he never missed a trick, and in general I think you were right but, in particular, I should say he missed several."

Green didn't comment, so after a brief pause, Masters continued: "Why didn't the prosecution attempt to prove a motive for the killing?"

"We're not bound to," said Hill.

"But you must admit that a motive helps to convince a jury and rounds a case off."

"Dammit, Chief, there wasn't one we could prove."

"Why not?"

"Because", said Sir Francis, taking over from Hill, "his wife had disinherited him weeks before. He knew it, because his wife told him. Her solicitor confirmed that fact in the box, so there wasn't a hope in hell of trying to prove financial gain. As for hatred and jealousy, we had no scrap of proof. Sex—he admitted he and his wife were no longer living as man and wife and said how he regretted it. And nobody has been able to find another woman. Hell's bells, George, there was no motive to suggest other than the financial one, and that was a non-starter."

"Then how is it that the man who never missed a trick failed to play the biggest card in his hand?"

"How do you mean?"

"Failed to point out that *you*, the prosecution, could suggest no motive."

"Hold it, hold it," growled Green. "Let me get this straight. You are saying, George, that not only did Connal not say that he had no motive, but he avoided mentioning to the court that the prosecution couldn't even suggest one, let alone prove it? Is that right?"

"Yes."

"But he did," exclaimed Hill. "He said he wouldn't be getting his wife's money, and . . ."

"Wrong, laddie," said Green. "If you read the court proceedings you'll see that it was Cuddles Cudlip who drew that out of him. Connal said nothing about it when he wasn't being led. Cudlip had to ask him if he profited in any material way from his wife's death, and it was only then that he said, 'No. My wife had cut me out of her will as a preliminary to divorce.' And that, chum, is the only disclaimer he made. Oh, I know he went on with a lot of taradiddle about insurance companies not paying up, but that had nothing to do with motive."

March said slowly: "You remembered all that?"

"Good memory," grunted Green, pleased by the implied compliment.

March turned to Masters. "Go on, George. It's beginning to sound interesting. Connal missed two chances. One, to say there was no motive and, two, to emphasise we hadn't suggested one."

"He said everything else," said Masters. "Played on every emotion, dredged up every little scrap of fact—or fiction—that could tell in his favour, but at no time did he play those two trump cards. I find that a curious omission in so polished a performance. If he had hinted—taunted the prosecution with not even suggesting a motive, let alone proving one—he'd really have convinced the jury of his innocence. He'd have nailed the coffin lid on your case, Frank, before you even got up to cross-examine."

There was a moment of silence.

"It is curious," admitted March.

Hill asked: "Why did he leave those two chances out, Chief?"

"If he is guilty—and I am assuming he is—I believe it was

because that particular point is his tender spot—the bit he wasn't quite sure of—an area he didn't want to draw attention to."

Green said: "I'm buying that. Nobody here is going to accept that a clever, calculating man like Connal is going to jeopardise his freedom for a motiveless murder. In fact, I'd say he's not the type to risk life imprisonment without a very powerful motive."

"I agree," said March, "but I wish I knew what his motive was. He's as smooth as cream on velvet. Whatever it was, he's kept it well hidden. So, having agreed he had a motive, what do you think it was, George? Are you going to be able to tell us?"

"Shall we work through it slowly?"

"As you please."

"Right. Next question. Why kill his wife before an imminent divorce? To me, that suggests that timing was significant."

"I don't get you, Chief."

"If timing was significant—or important, if you like—it would suggest to me that the murder had to be committed *before* the divorce, but *after* Mrs Connal's will had been changed."

"I still don't get it, Chief. Didn't it just happen that way?"

Masters explained quietly: "Once he was divorced from her, Connal could have had no claim to his wife's considerable fortune. So he had to murder her before the divorce could take place."

Hill still looked bewildered.

"Look, matey," said Green, "if he'd done her in before she'd disinherited him, he'd have had a motive as big as the Queen Mary. 'He wanted her money' is what you and Sir Francis would have said, and the jury would have believed you."

Before Hill could think of how to word the question he was obviously anxious to ask, March said: "You're a clever devil, George."

Masters relit his pipe. He could see that Hill was still struggling to grasp the point and was growing red in the face with embarrassment at being odd man out. He decided to rescue him. He asked the local D.I.: "What do you think will happen if Connal is acquitted?"

"He'll go free, Chief."

"That, certainly. But there's something else. Wouldn't you say

84

he'd be in a beautiful position to contest his wife's will? Latham, the solicitor, specifically told the court that the will had been changed solely because Angela Connal thought her husband was being unfaithful to her. But this murder trial—so far, at any rate—is proving that her attitude was based on misapprehension. Even the police have to agree with this, because we've not been able to trace Elizabeth Leacholt or any other woman in Connal's life. So Connal, if set free, will be able to plead that the new will, based on false premises, should be set aside, and that the former one—which left him his wife's entire estate—should stand." Masters turned to Sir Francis. "What would his chances be in law, Frank?"

"As you have just stated it, they would be nil. It's a good theory, George, but it is bad in law. Angela Connal's last will would stand even though the dispositions arose from misconceptions about her husband's behaviour."

"You could have fooled me," said Hill. "Even the Chief thought . . ."

"Ninety-nine people out of a hundred would probably think the same way as you two—in the absence of evidence as to her mental state. But in my view the second will would not be set aside even if Connal is acquitted of his wife's murder."

"That's put paid to the Chief's theory," said Hill.

"Nuts," said Green. "Look, laddo, we're here trying to pull your chestnuts out of the fire and you're spending your time pushing them back in again. Don't listen too hard to what Sir Frank says. He's a lawyer and can't see anything except from a strictly legal viewpoint."

"But . . ." Hill tried to interrupt, but Green pressed on.

"Take the realistic view, laddie. Why shouldn't what His Nibs has put forward be exactly Connal's motive? He could have believed he was in the right. I thought he was, His Nibs thought so, and so did you. Sir Frank says ninety-nine out of a hundred laymen would have thought so. It's almost certain Connal thought so. He isn't a lawyer and you could hardly say he was in a position to get legal advice on the point, could you?"

"I suppose not."

"I'll accept that, too," said March. "He had a motive, but it was based on false premises."

"Don't go too far too fast, Frank," counselled Masters. "Cast your mind back to Connal's evidence again. All the time he was in the box he was stressing his wife's longstanding state of depression and anxiety. To me—and I suspect to the jury—it seems as though he has been trying to establish that his wife was not in a fit mental state when she altered her will. If he gets off, and the jury believes what he is trying to suggest—that his wife committed suicide while mentally unstable—he would stand a good chance of getting the will changed even by your legal criteria."

March nodded. "You believe that Connal regards this case not as his own trial for murder, but merely as a powerful means of preparing the ground for contesting his wife's will?"

Hill cursed. "The crafty bastard." He turned to Green. "I told you what he was like, didn't I?"

"You didn't tell me half of it," growled Green.

"What about a drink before lunch?" suggested March.

When they reassembled after the meal, Masters asked: "Can we assume that what has so far been agreed should be our working hypothesis, even though we have no proof?"

"Suits me," said Green. "I've heard it said that every murderer makes one mistake, though in my experience they usually make a capful. Just to satisfy the legal profession we'll call this Connal's one mistake and take it from there."

"I'm agreed," said March readily. "As long as you put it that way and bear in mind that it is only a hypothesis based on a mistake."

Hill obviously would have preferred hard facts and proof to go with them. He said so, more in hope than as a complaint.

"If we accept it as a working basis," said Masters gently, "we can go on with the jigsaw—start to make other assumptions if you like to put it that way. But we are being forced to cut corners, you know. Lack of time could be our biggest problem, in fact."

Hill's agreement was tacit. March asked: "What other assumptions, George?"

"The obvious corollary is that Connal planned and executed the business of setting fire to his house with . . ."

"We started with that, Chief," complained Hill. "We're going round in circles."

"Hear me out, please. I say he planned the fire with extreme care. He knew that, as next of kin, the police would look at him very closely. So why not encourage them by giving them an apparently easy case? A superficial case, if you like."

"Superficial? You mean one that could easily be brought against him and then just as easily demolished at the trial?"

"Yes, Frank. Just that. Not to mince matters, I think you and Hill have been used. You were intended to be part of Connal's plan."

"You mean that he had to be arrested for murder and then cleared of the charge for his scheme to work?"

"As it was doing up till six o'clock last night," said Green. "He'll be lying in bed enjoying a nap this afternoon, will Connal. As sure as hell of himself and fully expecting to be free by teatime on Monday."

"Expecting?" asked Hill. "He could well be."

"Perhaps," said Masters cheerfully, "but I think we ought to be able to stop him. Frank, I'd like to go over the ground we've already covered, to draw the strands together and to see if there's anything more we can glean at this point."

"Fire away, George."

"This is how I see his plan. He had to ensure that his wife disinherited him and that she then started divorce proceedings."

"Ensure?" asked March incredulously. "You do realise what you said, don't you?"

"Patience, Frank. Judging by his testimony, I'd say Connal fancied himself as a bit of an amateur head-shrinker. He dabbled in psychology quite a bit, I think. He'd got his wife's condition pretty well weighed up, and so he could foresee her probable reactions to anything he might do. He could, therefore, goad her into taking the steps she actually took. At any rate, he knew that after he sent her that first anonymous letter . . ."

"What!" exclaimed an outraged Hill. "Are you saying, Chief,

87

that he actually wrote the letter defaming himself to his own wife?"

"Feel for the bedpost, lad," chided Green. "What else? Otherwise, why, despite a massive police search directed by you personally, do you think this Leacholt bird hasn't been discovered? After all, it's an uncommon name and so not one that could remain hidden for long. That's why Connal chose it. I'll bet he worked hard and long selecting it, too."

There was a moment of silence, while Hill and Sir Francis assimilated this. At the end of it, Green apparently didn't feel satisfied that they had fully grasped the point.

"Look, matey," he said, offering Hill his battered packet of Kensitas, "you know well enough that if a poison-pen maniac had sent that letter, he'd have sent an anonymous note to the police after Angela Connal's death. It's a known fact that those gents don't know when to stop, and whichever of the Connals he had it in for . . ."

"How do you mean?"

"If a poison-pen writer sent that letter to Angela Connal, was he trying to hurt her or to do her husband one in the eye?"

"I don't know. How could I?"

"I'm not saying you could, lad. All I'm saying is that whichever it was, he'd never have missed the chance that the fire gave him to poop off a few more missiles."

"I get you. If he'd had it in for Mrs Connal, he'd have written to me to say something like 'The bitch got her just deserts', or if he'd had it in for Connal himself, the message would have said 'He murdered his wife.'"

"You're learning fast," said Green in mock admiration.

Hill shook his head in amazement. Since leaving Masters' team he had met little professionalism of this sort. Nowadays—on his own—he was accustomed to working by the book—stolidly. Despite his training with Masters, it was doubtful whether he had ever heard of the First Cause: that for every action there was an underlying cause or reason and that, to get at it, one had to dig below the surface, and sometimes dig so deep as to be almost beyond human comprehension. Hill was not a more superficial man than most. His religious belief would cause him to agree fervently that God made the universe, but ask him who or what made God in the first place and he'd be lost. Masters had—as it were—always asked who or what made God. It had brought surprisingly successful results in crime investigation. A man killed from fear. What caused the fear? Answering that question led to an understanding not only of the crime, but of the person who had committed it.

March, as the onlooker, understood Hill's amazement, and felt that it would not help to have the local man feel too far out of his depth. "Cheer up, Mr Hill. You should know how George Masters works."

"I do know," retorted Hill, "and I accepted and appreciated his methods when I worked with him. But in those days he was carrying the can and he always based everything on known fact. This time it's my case, and he's playing guessing games."

"Of course I am, in a way," confessed Masters. "But you did agree that I should assume Connal's guilt—on your say so. True?"

"Yes, Chief."

"For me to be asked to investigate a case after the criminal has been arrested and charged is an oddity. And that, I claim, allows me to use odd—unusual, if you like—methods. We're all out of our depth, because we're doing a job arse-about-face and so, where we would normally get facts and then make deductions, I now have to make deductions and hope that as a result I get facts. So let me hypothesise and then see if what I come up with touches ground somewhere."

"Sorry, Chief," said Hill.

"Nothing to be sorry about, lad," said Green. "You hold your corner for as long as you want. I don't suppose you've had so many murder investigations of your own that a failure wouldn't bother you. But His Nibs is making sense to me, if that's any comfort to you."

"As I was saying," said Masters, who seemed anxious to press ahead, "Connal guessed that his wife would want to hit back after she received that letter. It was a predictable reaction, in so far as the two usual reactions on the part of a wronged wife are either sorrow or anger. It was merely a matter of deciding—from experience—which would be Mrs Connal's likely reaction and then of considering what course her anger would drive her to adopt."

"I'm with you," said Hill, with relief in his voice. "You're saying, Chief, that Connal's guess would be an easy one, because when a rich wife contributes much of the upkeep in a household, her first thought if she is angry and wants to kick hubby in the pants must, inevitably, be the decision to cut off the money supply."

"That's the general idea, though whether Mrs Connal helped with the upkeep of the house is doubtful, because Connal himself must have been getting a big salary. What I think is that changing her will and suing for divorce were the two most obvious courses open to Mrs Connal. The former was an immediate, intensely satisfying step. Suing for divorce is a longer-term business and obviously she would need more evidence than one anonymous letter. So, to begin with, she just changed her will as, I believe, Connal intended she should."

Sir Francis said: "If she hadn't done so, she would still be alive. That's a conclusion so outrageous that nobody in his right mind would ever arrive at it."

"Thank you very much, Frank."

"Sorry, George, but you must admit it is unbelievable to ordinary mortals. Simple souls like me who prosecute the biggest villains in the country would expect a woman to die if she hadn't cut her husband out of her will."

"If you'll stop gossiping . . ."

"Gossiping! My dear George!"

Masters turned to Hill. "After he was told his wife had changed her will, Connal visited Latham. Why do you think he did that?"

"Why, Chief? To do what you talked about a few minutes ago. To drag out of the solicitor one fact—an admission that Mrs Connal had changed her will as a direct result of receiving the anonymous letter."

"Excellent. So now tell me why that admission was so important to Connal."

"He thought he needed it as evidence if he was later to contest the will with any chance of success."

"Correct. What deductions does that assumption lead you to make?"

Hill hesitated a moment or two in deep thought. Green said encouragingly: "Come on, matey. Have a bash."

At last Hill was ready to speak. "Two deductions, Chief. Having got Latham to agree that point, by labouring it—and he mentioned it twice in court, I think—Connal could then go ahead and give his wife more grounds for starting a divorce suit. And if he wrote the letter, then he must have provided that nude picture. He planted it on himself where he knew it would be found and would then be taken to Latham as a reason for starting the divorce."

"Right. Second deduction?"

"Once he had Latham's assurances about the reason for the will being changed and the fact that a divorce suit was actually being filed, Connal could go ahead with his preparations for the actual murder—knowing for sure it was on."

"Full marks."

"So the girlie picture was another bit of his clever work," said March sourly.

"The act of putting it where he knew it would be found come suit cleaning time was, superficially, clever," admitted Masters, "but I think it was another of his mistakes."

"Really? It served its purpose. It caused his wife to start divorce proceedings. Eminently successful."

"In that way, it was. But I'm using his testimony as killing ground, remember. I said he missed several tricks. This is another of them."

"The card itself? Or what he had to say about it?"

"What he didn't say about it. Another error of omission. He didn't mention in his evidence that the police had not found his fingerprints on the picture."

"Cripes," said Green. "I hadn't thought of that one."

"Which one?" asked Hill.

"Why should he have mentioned it?" asked Sir Francis.

"Because it would have been another strong point in his favour if he had said so. And believe me, a man who had never touched that photograph would have said so with all the earnestness and simplicity of innocence. Any man would have done so, let alone one as smart as Connal."

"Then why didn't he mention it, Chief?" asked Hill. "He knew we'd tested it and not found his dabs on it. Actually we only found four sets—Mrs Connal, Mrs King, Mr Latham and his private detective."

"He daren't mention it," said Green scathingly. "It had been wiped, hadn't it?"

"That's right."

"But you didn't tell the defence that it had been wiped, did you?"

"Of course not."

"Then how did he know?"

"Know what?"

Green expired loudly. "There are two facts about that nude. One, that certain dabs had been lifted from the picture of her lily-white torso and, two, that the whole job had been wiped sometime previously. You had to inform the defence that Connal's prints were not among those you lifted from the snap. But you were in no way obliged to give them the negative piece of information that the photo had been wiped. So you didn't tell them. Right?"

"Right. But I still don't see what you're getting at."

"A clever bastard like Connal would have chucked it in your face that you didn't find his prints—if he'd dared. So why daren't he? The only reason could be because he knew the bloody portrait had been wiped. And if you didn't tell him it had been wiped, how could he possibly know it had been?"

"I know all that," said Hill, "but what good would it have done the prosecution if he had introduced it?"

Masters felt it was time to intervene. "The fact that he *didn't* mention a point that would have told in his favour is a strong indication that Connal fought shy of making it because he *had* handled the photograph and he *had* wiped it himself. That is the first point. The second is that Sir Francis could have made quite a few telling remarks about the difficulty of insinuating a dabless

92

photograph into a stranger's pocket, whereas it would be just too easy for the owner of the jacket to do it himself."

March grimaced. "Actually, I did intend to mention the photograph. But unlike you, I didn't visualise it as a positive point. My intention was to stress its negative value."

"I'm sure you were, Frank. But on Monday you've got two strings for that particular bow."

March nodded.

"How about a cup of tea, now?" I think we could all do with a break."

CHAPTER V

WHEN THEY WERE again sitting round the table after the half-hour break that Sir Francis had insisted on, Masters said: "Just to link up with our last session, can we agree that the photograph was planted specifically to give Latham something to work on—to get his private detective to look into? If so, it means we can accept that Connal wanted his wife to start divorce proceedings, even if only tentatively. That, in turn, supports our assumption that the murder was planned to come *after* the will had been changed and the divorce suit was under way, but *before* the divorce was brought to court."

Nobody disagreed, but Hill asked: "What about the cheque to Gladys Robertson? That only came to light right at the last minute."

"Of course it did. Isn't that what you would have expected? You see, the cheque was genuine, and could have been proved so by Latham very quickly, so it wouldn't have helped him in the divorce suit."

"You mean it wasn't intended to?"

"I believe it was introduced to provide Connal with a strong, sympathy-rousing 'out' in the eyes of any jury he might subsequently have had to face. He said in court that he saw no reason to mention the gift to his wife. Utter rot! Men who run around handing out from their joint accounts cheques for five hundred quid to other females, make a point of telling their wives about such gifts—if only to avoid misunderstanding later."

"But," said Hill, "Connal only got to know that the cheque had turned up that last morning."

"No, no, Mr Hill," said Sir Francis.

"No?"

94

"Of course not," said Masters. "Connal went off that day before the postman had arrived. The cheques must have reached Ashbury House from the bank at least the day before, if not several days before. Connal would know they were there—he would have seen the distinctive bank envelope on the breakfast table or lying about the house somewhere. Besides, his wife told him that last morning that she had already given Latham the cheque as evidence. I think he knew that before she told him."

"You mean he waited until he knew that that particular cheque had gone from the pile before he made any further move?" asked Hill.

"Precisely. And so the stage was set for murder," said Sir Francis quietly.

Hill shrugged. "We all know the Chief is right. But we've still got no hard facts. Only clever speculation."

"Cheer up," replied Masters. "We haven't finished yet. And I have a feeling your friend the milkman is going to help us. Can you get him here, now?"

Not only Hill, but Sir Francis, too, looked astounded. "Bill Parker?" gasped Hill. "He'd nothing to give us. Sir Francis only cross-examined at length in the hope of gaining a bit of time."

"Sheer waffle," admitted March.

"You did better than you know, Frank."

"I'm pleased to hear it. How can he help us?"

"You'll learn when he gets here."

Hill pushed his seat back. "In that case my people may as well bring him in. Up here, Chief?"

"If you please."

It was after six when Hill's D.C. knocked on the door and the milkman was shown into the hotel suite.

"Sit down, Mr Parker," said March. "You and I played a little question and answer game yesterday afternoon. Not too bad, was it?"

Parker grinned. He was a paunchy man, not very tall. His face was weather-beaten and cheerful. His teeth were bad, but they seemed to be so right for his features that they did not detract from his jollity. It was obvious he was in good humour. His reply said so.

"I enjoyed it, sir. New experience for me, that was. 'Course, I've seen it on the telly and wondered what it would be like in the flesh, as you might say. But not too bad at all, it wasn't."

"Fine. Detective Chief Superintendent Masters would like to ask you a few more questions. I don't think they'll be any more difficult than mine were. But before you begin, would you like a whisky?"

"Never say no to a Scotch, sir, even though I do spend my life selling pintas."

After these preliminaries, Masters felt free to start.

"I was particularly interested in one thing you said in evidence, Mr Parker. That was that you left three pints of milk at Ashbury House on the day of the fire, but that you had never left that number before."

"Yeah, odd that, wasn't it? Seems to have marked the occasion, you might say."

"You are positive that there was no other occasion on which you left three pints?"

"Not according to my book and my memory there never was."

"You've looked at your book?"

"I did that. 'Course it only goes back to the first of Jan this year, this one. But my old 'uns'll tell you the same thing if they've still got 'em at the depot."

"I'm sure we'll find what you say is true. Memory doesn't let a chap like you down."

"Not with the regular regulars as you might call them. Two usually at Ashbury House, with a large carton of cream on big party days. But never three. Sort of coincidence or something you might say."

Masters was rubbing Warlock Flake in his left palm with the heel of his right hand. He didn't look up as he said: "I'm also interested in knowing why you think you were asked to leave three pints on that particular day."

Parker rasped stubby fingers across a chin which by this time in the evening was bristly enough to show that he had probably shaved before beginning his rounds in the early hours of the day.

96

"Easy," he replied. "They'd run right out. Normally—in a house as well run as that one—they have one bottle left over from the day before, and just buy two to top up, like. So I guessed they'd run right out for some reason and had to over-order on the day of the fire."

"I see. But don't you think—looking back on it—that it was rather odder than odd that at a time when the household was reduced by the absence of Mrs King, they should require more milk than they had ever done before?"

Parker scratched one ear. "Now you come to mention it, yes I do. But I hadn't looked at it that way. Odder than odd, eh? I must tell my missus that."

Sir Francis raised one hand slightly, as if asking permission to speak.

"Yes, Frank?"

"I just wanted to say to Mr Hill that this is the point that has been niggling me ever since yesterday afternoon. Not that I had worked it out as you have, George, but I half picked it up and then later couldn't remember what it was that had caused the momentary ripple on the sludge of my brain. It was the point that two pints was the usual amount for three people, but on the day of the fire it was three pints for two."

Hill grinned. "It's as well you remembered it, Sir Francis, or you'd have been left wondering for ever. And, incidentally, Chief, it was the fact that Sir Francis couldn't remember that point that really decided us to ask for your help."

"Ah, well," said Green, "it's nice to know that a couple of senior blokes from the Yard are asked to give up their weekend off to trace a missing bottle of cow juice."

"It wasn't like that at all . . ." began Hill.

"Ignore the D.C.I.," counselled Masters before turning back to the roundsman.

"Thank you, Mr Parker. That's all I wanted to ask you."

The milkman was surprised, and he was not alone. March and Hill both seemed astounded.

"There is one thing we'd like you to do, Bill, mate," said Green.

"What's that?"

"Take your delivery book to the nick to be photocopied. A cop-car will take you home and back."

"Right, sir. As long as they don't want to keep the book. Thanks for the Scotch and bye-bye all."

When Parker had gone, March turned to Masters. "What does it all mean, George?"

Hill said: "Picking the poor bloke up on a Saturday night and bringing him in here just for that! We could have worked it all out without keeping him from his pub."

"You wanted evidence, laddo," said Green.

"There's no evidence there we haven't already got."

"Ah! But what conclusions did you draw from it in court? Sir Francis only went on and on about that milk to prolong the agony a bit and waste time, and when the judge asked him if the amount of milk delivered was important to the Crown's case, he said 'Not fundamentally, m'lud.'"

"Quite right, I did."

"So keep your shirt on, young Hilly, and listen to His Nibs."

"Surely you see the value of all this?" said Masters plaintively, and applied another match to his pipe.

"No," said March, "we don't—although we feel it is important."

Masters shrugged. "Mrs Brignell said that while they were talking on the front doorstep, she overheard Connal tell his wife to take a glass of warm milk and her pills and go back to bed."

"What's odd about that, Chief? She always did, apparently."

"Then why should Connal bother to mention it?"

Hill considered this a moment, knowing that Masters had some point he wished to have dragged out of obscurity. Then the light dawned. He said: "I'm beginning to see what you mean, Chief. If she was so short of milk that she had to go out and alter the indicator to three that morning, after having thought there was enough in the house only to order two the night before, it means that either Angela Connal had made a wrong estimate or some of the milk had mysteriously disappeared."

March crowed with delight. "Got it, George. Connal poured it all away except for one half-pint which he knew his wife would need and which he therefore doctored with knock-out drops of some sort."

Masters nodded. "I believe he made sure she would have no other milk to use except the half-pint he'd laced with something to make her sleep like a log."

"Through all the clatter and rumpus of a fire like that?" breathed Hill. "It's obscene. It's worse . . . it . . ."

"It gels," said Green. "That's the important thing now. It has to. Think, laddo. Even though you may beef that there are no hard facts yet, you must agree it was too much of a coincidence for the house to need three pints for the first time ever on the day it was burnt down and when there were fewer people living there. It must have significance. Surely you can see it happening, can't you? Mrs C. goes to the fridge for her cow-juice and sees she has only halfa pinta left. She puts that in the pan to warm up, goes to the side door to alter the clock to ask for an extra bottle, locks and chains the doors, puts her milk into a glass in one of those little holders, goes up to bed, drinks the milk and takes her pills, settles back and bingo! Nothing on earth would wake her. Nothing ever did, again."

"It's diabolical," said Hill. "Christ! If only we'd got something to nail the bastard with on Monday morning."

Masters eased his bulk in the small chair. "We're working our way through it, Hill. Filling in the picture. That's the only way the material facts will come."

"I hope so, Chief."

"Now for the next little bit. Shoot me down if you think I'm getting fanciful."

"Fanciful? You? Never let it be said, George. Anybody who accused you of anything like that would be out of his mind." Green turned to March. "I'm right, aren't I?"

"He does get the oddest ideas about himself, doesn't he?" March's grin robbed the remark of any sting.

Green got to his feet. "I'm going to ask them to send up some beer, if you don't mind, Sir Frank."

"Go ahead."

99

"You can pay for it out of your slush fund," Green said to Hill. "Payment for information received, unaccounted for by name."

Hill nodded his agreement.

"Mrs Connal was, by all accounts, a sensible woman despite her undoubted anxiety," said Masters. "Yet she decided to take drastic action to the tune of cutting her husband out of her will after receiving just one anonymous letter. Earlier on, I made capital out of this fact, in so far as I argued that her husband foresaw exactly this reaction. Connal foresaw it correctly, because he knew his wife so well. But what was Latham's reaction when she approached him with such flimsy evidence of infidelity? Frank, I know you are not a family solicitor, but you are a lawyer. Put yourself in the shoes of a family man-of-affairs and tell us what you would have said and done in Latham's place."

"Cor!" said the eminent Q.C., playing for a moment or two in which to decide on his answer. "You do ask awkward questions, George."

"So do you. You make a habit of it and a living out of it. So—answer, please."

"Bearing in mind that adultery is practically discounted in divorce courts these days, I'd have felt obliged to head her off any such drastic action on such slim grounds."

"Including changing a will?"

"Yes. Because I would suggest that changing a will in these circumstances was an action which could not stand alone. It would have to be the preliminary to divorce. No couple like the Connals could have continued to live together with that change of will between them. That's why I said that bit about adultery being less important today. Of course, as we all know, a will can be changed at any time and there need be no excuse for doing it, but I think a good solicitor would have urged some delay—a sort of cooling-off period—when a will was to be changed for so unauthenticated a reason as that letter. I'm sure that Latham—judging by what I've seen of him—would have done just that. Otherwise, in my opinion, he would have been failing in his duty."

"In spite of what you've said, Frank, Mrs Connal did take precipitate action, aided and—in so far as the new will was prepared and signed on the same day—abetted by Latham. What conclusion do you draw from that?"

"I can only think that she told Latham something more to her husband's discredit. Something which, together with the anonymous letter, caused him to act with unusual haste over preparing the new will and, later, when the nude picture came along, over instituting divorce proceedings."

"That's exactly what I hoped you'd say," said Masters. "These days, though a woman may not exactly approve her husband's sexual promiscuity, she won't normally react to an anonymous hint to quite such a degree as Mrs Connal seems to have done, unless there are supporting reasons. Did either of you two who were in court get any hint of this in Latham's testimony? I seem to remember in the text it was short, dry and factual."

"I saw him several times before the trial," said Hill, "but he gave me no hint at all."

"We got no suggestion that there were any underlying reasons for his client's actions," said March.

"Then we've got to get Latham here and get him to tell us anything there might be."

"You can't do that, Chief," said Hill. "A legal confidence is sacrosanct and can't be broken."

Green said: "Be your age, laddo! That claptrap only applies so long as both parties wish it to be so. In this case, one party is dead, so the other can come across with any secrets he sees fit to disclose."

Hill looked at March. "Is that the law, Sir Francis?"

"I wouldn't like to give an opinion on it without reference, but it sounds logical enough."

"I'm sure Latham will agree," urged Masters, "so long as we only ask him for information that has a direct bearing on the case. Ring and ask him if he would be kind enough to come round to the hotel, please."

"It's Saturday night. Nearly dinnertime," said Hill doubtfully.

"Come on," growled Green. "Where's all that willingness to work every hour that God sends if it helps to nail Connal?"

"I'll speak to him," said March. "He'll probably be more

willing to put himself out for me than you others. Brothers-in-Law, you see. I'll suggest after dinner, because it's time we were eating, too."

"Beautiful bit of lamb," said Green, wiping his mouth with his napkin.

"Let me ask for some more for you, Mr Green. Mr Hill?"

"Ta!" said Green.

"Not for me, thank you," said Hill. "I'd rather return to our own particular muttons."

"Can you hold it until we're back in my suite? I don't think we're out of earshot. The trouble with Elmhurst is that we don't establish a Mess because it's so near London. Most counsel commute to and fro daily. The consequence is that those who do stay tend to treat this dining room as their own, and linger at table."

"Anybody in particular who shouldn't overhear?"

"Cudlip's junior. Ockenshaw. He's about eight feet to your south-west, with large red ears cocked like those of a terrier expecting a doggy-choc."

The dining room was the best part of the hotel. It had been enlarged and refurbished as the first part of a programme to give the building some right to the claim to be Elmhurst's leading pub. No doubt the establishment of a new, popular, chain-store type of eating house almost next door had caused the hotel management to concentrate on their dining room, kitchen and chefs before all else. The food was very eatable, the lighting suitably dim, the furniture reasonably well reproduced and the cutlery not too garishly stainless steel. One of Masters' pet hates was cutlery stamped out of a sheet of metal no more than fifty thousandths of an inch thick. He liked his eating irons solid, with a bit of craftsmanship displayed in the making.

"Is he really trying to overhear us?"

"If not, he is unquestionably interested in the fact that I have three eminent policemen as guests."

"He obviously knows Hill. But Green and myself. . . ?"

Sir Francis laughed. "Modesty, George? There's no member of any Inn that doesn't know you and Mr Green by sight or reputation. Green there has a bit of a name up, you know, for some devastatingly down-to-earth replies under cross-examination."

Masters grinned. Green had begun to make a reputation for himself when he had described one prisoner as a bar-steward. Defence counsel had protested, but the judge had seen no reason to interfere as, technically, the description could not be faulted. This success had been like heady wine to Green who had often suffered in the war of accusatory semantics waged on police witnesses by some counsel. The D.C.I. had gone from strength to strength. Masters privately believed that Green thought up some similar reply in advance of any trial and somehow worked his witticism in, much as Churchill is reputed to have steered parliamentary debates so that he might, without appearing irrelevant, let loose some carefully prepared verbal shaft.

"By the way," said Sir Francis, accepting more mint sauce from Masters, "you didn't tell me why you brought Mr Green with you. We're delighted to have him and to make use of his services, but Hill and I did explain it was a private kindness we were seeking."

Green edged a strand of lamb from between two teeth with a finger nail and then answered in place of Masters who had a mouthful.

"When His Nibs realised it was Crown counsel wanting a bit of help on the old-boy basis as well as our old pal here calling on us to come and hold his hand, he reckoned it should be done D.O. The two of us, but no sergeants."

"D.O.?" asked Hill. "I've never come across that."

"Demi-official, matey."

"Why not semi-official?"

Sir Francis put his knife and fork together and sat back. "Because semi means, roughly speaking, exactly half—as for instance in semicircle. Demi, I suppose, should mean the same, but for some reason or another, in the service of the Crown, we regard demi as meaning 'diminutive', 'curtailed' or—quite often—'in combination'. I think the use is a throwback to arms and armour, as in demi-cuirass; or to heraldry, as in demilion, demi-vol and so on. Did you know that what is today called a coronet was at one time a demi crown—a diminutive or small crown, where a semi crown might just conceivably have been a full sized crown chopped in half. . . . Ah! Ockenshaw is on his way. Sorry for talking nonsense whilst he was about, but we can get down to our real business over cheese and coffee if you wish."

As Latham had agreed to come at March's invitation, it was natural to leave the Q.C. the business of explaining to the solicitor not only the presence of the two Yard men but also the reason for the invitation and what was wanted of him.

"Sorry to drag you out as late as this on a Saturday, Latham, but Detective Chief Superintendent Masters and Detective Chief Inspector Green have produced important new evidence in the Connal case. So much so that we are now able to reconstruct, in considerable detail, the events leading up to the tragedy. Some bits are, however, either missing or in need of confirmation. One of them, we think, concerns you. We have very little time at our disposal between now and Monday morning, so we hope you will agree to help us."

Latham accepted neat whisky. He sipped it for a moment while considering his reply.

"I knew Angela Connal from childhood, Sir Francis. She was a few years younger than I am, but I watched her grow up. Not to mince matters, I was a sadly disappointed man when she preferred Connal to me. But we were close friends until her death."

"Thank you for that confidence. May we take it that if we give you our assurance that what we are asking is aimed solely at bringing his crime home to her murderer, we shall have your help?"

"I left the court last evening a dissatisfied man—sure in my own mind that he has got away with it."

"That is precisely the reason for our activity tonight. Masters and Green have been here all day, giving Hill and myself the benefit of their great investigational skills."

"In that case, Sir Francis, please ask your questions. I can always refuse to answer any I may consider improper."

"You have that right. I hope you will exercise it to the full should any of us here overstep the mark."

"Brothers-in-Law!" whispered Green to Masters. "They're like a couple of heavyweights manoeuvring for positions in a ring."

Latham inclined his head in agreement with March who then turned to Masters with a mute sign to begin. Masters took his time. He had summed up Latham as fully prepared to co-operate, but also as such a cautious bird by nature that he might well have qualms about the rectitude of agreeing to be questioned along new lines in the middle of a trial. Masters knew that Latham would agree that it is the duty of both sides to continue to dig up fresh evidence right until the last moment in court, but the solicitor gave the impression that he doubted the wisdom of being involved in such an exercise himself, particularly at so late a stage in the trial.

"Mr Latham, we have come to the conclusion that you would have refused to act in the matter of a precipitate redrafting of Mrs Connal's will and an almost equally rapid filing of a divorce suit based solely on the flimsy evidence provided by an unsigned letter and naughty photograph. Are we correct in that conclusion?"

"Yes, Mr Masters, you are. Not that I would have gone to the lengths of refusing to act where a valued client and friend such as Mrs Connal was concerned, but I most certainly would have advised very strongly against anything but long-considered action."

"Thank you. Your reply suggests to me that Mrs Connal must have presented you with other evidence sufficiently detrimental to her husband to cause you to agree to act. If I am right, are you prepared to tell us what that evidence was?"

Latham sipped his whisky. He was obviously not prepared to speak without prior thought. Masters noticed that as he put his glass down, his jaws were working. An indication of strength of will? The Chief Superintendent guessed that once this man had made a decision, he would stick to it. This moment of silence, therefore, was crucial. Latham was weighing privately whether to help or to lapse into professional rectitude.

At last his mind was made up.

"It was not evidence."

Masters' relief was in no way lessened by this statement, but he asked: "Not evidence? You are saying there were no facts on which to base the action you took?"

"Only one fact—fear. The cause of her fear was not fact even though I had no hesitation in accepting it as a valid reason to act. Valid because, though what Angela recounted to me was only an impression held by a nervous woman who had been severely shaken by an anonymous letter, she was undeniably a frightened woman. Her fear was fact—the reason for it was not."

"You appear to suggest that what you heard should have been discounted because the account was merely that of an impression, presumably received sometime earlier. Further, because, when she spoke to you, Mrs Connal was under great stress—coming on top of what I gather from the evidence in court was a permanent state of mild anxiety—you suggest that you should have been a little sceptical of what you were told. Yet you acted immediately. Am I right?"

"Yes. I acted because, as I told you, Angela told me the letter had frightened her."

"In what way had it frightened her?"

"She could give me no precise reason for the fear. And despite her tension headaches, Mrs Connal was a level-headed, shrewd and, in my opinion, brave woman."

Green said: "You mean she wouldn't scare easily under any threat, let alone start to panic because she got an unsigned scandal note?"

"Quite. And it was because she did not panic and because she remained perfectly cool that I could place enough credence in—and therefore act upon—what she told me."

Masters asked: "What happened, Mr Latham?"

"Naturally I tried to fathom the reasons for her sudden fear and I was successful in so far as she told me of an impression she had held for some years."

Masters felt it was like drawing teeth to get this man really talking. So he decided to plunge, hoping to increase the pace and content of the conversation.

"I am guessing now. Did her impression concern her child?"

"Why do you ask that?" Latham had come alive. His question was faster, with more edge to it.

"Because from my reading of the evidence I came to the conclusion that it was not her father's death, but the unhappy and untimely death of her small son that really started Mrs Connal's mental and domestic troubles. I believe that everything that has followed must have stemmed from that tragedy."

"Right," grunted Green. "The old man's death was natural, the kid's was unnatural."

"You're a perspicacious man, Mr Masters."

"If I have stumbled on some of the truth, Mr Latham, may I not know it all?"

Latham inclined his head slightly in agreement before continuing.

"This, in brief, is what Angela told me that day when she brought the anonymous note into my office. Robin—her three-year-old son—was suffering from anaphylaxis which is, I believe, a state of shock due to some allergy. Be that as it may, the child was hypersensitive to something, but not being a doctor, I don't know the ins and outs of it."

"Don't worry about that bit, Mr Latham," said Masters. "But for the benefit of anybody present who does not know what anaphylactic shock is, perhaps I should just say that technically it is an unfortunate reaction after an injection. What it means, generally, is that a patient is given an injection of serum—as for tetanus or diphtheria—and reacts adversely because something—maybe a previous injection—has sensitised him. Sensitisation usually means that there is an absence of circulating antibody in the blood to counteract the infection caused by the second injection, and as a consequence there is an excess of histamine in the body. In other words, the body's natural defences are down—at any rate for a time."

"That's about as clear as mud," muttered Green. "Do you mean that the first jab doesn't do its job properly? That instead of protecting the body it weakens it in some way so that when the second lot comes along there's no defence against it and things go wrong?"

"That's it—roughly speaking."

"Was Robin very ill?" March asked Latham.

"Apparently he was, but the doctor believed—as the Chief Superintendent indicated—that it was only a matter of time before he recovered and he therefore preferred not to move him to hospital."

"Why?" asked March.

"Because," said Masters, "with the body defences down, the boy would have been susceptible to any infection there was about. A children's ward in a hospital can have all manner of infections which might not affect most kids, but which would be dangerous to one in Robin's condition. Remember, his defences were down."

"So the doctor made a right decision?"

"A logical one, certainly." Masters turned back to Latham. "Robin must have had some medicine."

"He was taking tablets with an antihistamine and a sedative in them, according to Angela."

"Do you happen to know what they were?"

"Angela couldn't remember their name. But she said they were tiny and pale blue in colour. Quite tasteless and easy to take. They would have to be, wouldn't they, if they were given to small children?"

Masters was thoughtful. Something had begun to click in his mind. He came to with a start to agree with Latham's question.

"Anyhow," continued the solicitor, "to cut the story short, Angela went to sleep when the boy started to recover. So much is fact, and you will have read about it in Connal's evidence."

"Yes."

"When she awoke to find the boy dead, Angela was obviously too shocked by the tragedy to appreciate what went on. She was led away from Robin's room by her husband, but everything about that room and its contents must have been etched on her mind without her realising it. I believe she had total recall of every item and every action in that room until the day she died."

"I can believe that," said March. "I've come across something similar before. We all have, to some extent. How many times have you heard a witness to a tragedy claim long after the event that he can still actively hear the sound of the crash, or still see exactly how a deadly event occurred? Partial recall only, of course, in the cases I've mentioned, but when it comes to a young mother and her very much loved only child . . . well, I'll believe she had total recall."

Latham went on: "It was not until later that the significance of certain things dawned on her. It was after she recovered from the initial shock that she recalled her first thought on waking that night."

Nobody spoke. They waited for Latham to take up his story again.

"It was that the child must have needed and been given more tablets during the time she had been asleep. She recalled thinking that the bottle of little pills was far emptier than it had been earlier."

It was said with a finality that was not lost on the listeners. It was Hill who could bear the silence least. He blurted out: "My God! You mean to say she thought Connal had killed his own son?"

Latham, a slight frown on his face, looked across at the Inspector. "It was the conclusion Angela arrived at."

"Latham," asked Sir Francis quietly, "did you know the family doctor?"

"Craddock? Of course I knew him."

"As an able doctor?"

"He is both highly qualified and highly regarded."

"Do you happen to know what his reactions were to his young patient's death?"

Latham nodded. "I can vouch for the fact that he signed the certificate with no doubts in his mind as to the cause of death, but he was a very shaken man. He had certainly not expected the child to die. He stated so at the inquest which I, of course, attended."

"Was there a second signature?"

"There was no need. Craddock had been in recent attendance on the child."

"A post-mortem?"

"It was not considered necessary. Death due to anaphylactic shock is not unknown, I understand."

Hill wasn't satisfied. He sounded disturbed as he spoke. "Mr Latham, you said that Dr Craddock who is, I know, a very conscientious and skilled doctor, had not expected the little boy to die. So why didn't he suspect foul play?"

Latham shrugged. Masters answered.

"Would you have suspected it with nobody there but the child's parents? Put yourself in Craddock's position. He was a worried man, but he had no reason to be a suspicious one. The child had been very ill. Every medical man meets these quirks of fate. Remission in a supposedly incurable patient; serious deterioration in a condition that seems to be going along nicely."

"But the bottle of tablets," said Hill wildly. "Surely to God he'd have known through counting them?"

"I wonder how often it occurs to a doctor to count pills after a patient has died? In front of a dead child's parents?" Masters shook his head. "It would be out of character. He would have needed to be very suspicious indeed even to think of it."

Latham said: "Angela told me that her husband had very solicitously cleared and straightened the bedroom before Craddock arrived."

Green growled: "Most people tidy up a bit if they know the doctor's coming. Did Mrs Connal say what happened to the pills? After her old man had taken them away?"

"Angela was so distraught at the time that she didn't pay attention to what became of them. All she knew was that they had disappeared from Robin's room. When she asked him later, Connal said he had thrown them away."

Masters got to his feet, pipe in hand. Everybody watched him closely.

"Will Craddock be in the local phone book?"

Latham nodded. "Of course. But I don't know whether he'll be at home at half-past ten on a Saturday night."

"Doctors have to leave addresses where they can be reached at any time."

Masters sounded curt. It was an indication that his thoughts were far from pleasant as he picked up the phone and asked the hotel switchboard to ring Craddock's number. His attitude was not much help when the doctor answered and, on hearing Masters' question, refused to give the information asked for—declining on ethical grounds.

"Ethical?" asked Masters menacingly. "What is there so ethical about saying which drug was given to a patient who died years ago?"

The reply was unintelligible to the others in the suite, but they were able to guess that Craddock, having retreated from his ethical stand, was now demurring on the grounds that he did not know Masters.

"Dr Craddock," asked Masters, "do you know either Detective Inspector Hill or alternatively Mr Latham, the late Mrs Connal's solicitor?"

"Latham, certainly."

"He is here with me now. If I put him on to you will you be good enough to let him know the answer?"

Craddock must have agreed. Masters held the phone out to Latham, who got to his feet. "Please take down the name of the drug, Mr Latham." He handed over a silver pencil and an envelope from his breast pocket.

It took Latham less than a couple of minutes to first reassure Craddock, and then take down the name spelled out to him.

"Promethazine hydrochloride," said Masters, taking the envelope when Latham had put the phone down. He frowned over the rest of the message which was in a scrawled longhand, unlike the name of the drug which had been printed as dictated. "Perhaps you would read your notes, Mr Latham."

"Sorry. I have a rotten fist. Particularly when taking phone messages. What Craddock said is that they were tiny tablets of ten milligrams for children. Bluish in colour. A child would take one or at the most two to settle it down. An adult would need at least fifty milligrams, or at least five tablets, to sedate. More would result in profound sleep."

Latham put the envelope on the table and resumed his seat. The others remained silent. After a pause, Masters again addressed the solicitor.

"Mr Latham, did you believe Mrs Connal when she told you her husband had cleared away the pills and other paraphernalia from the sick room? And when she told you her husband had declared he had disposed of the tablets?"

"Down the loo," said Green.

"Yes, I believed her."

"You didn't seek to authenticate the statement in any way?"

"For a moment or two, as Angela was giving me her account of what happened that night, I thought it might have been the figment of a fevered imagination. But the child *did* die unexpectedly and the pills *did* disappear."

"Did they? We have no proof that they did."

"You can, of course, doubt Mrs Connal's word . . ." Latham sounded huffed, so Masters hastened to remove the wrong impression he had given.

"Not at all. You misunderstand me. What I am asking is, could Connal have told his wife he had disposed of them, but have kept them for subsequent use?"

Sir Francis answered. "He could. They could have been crushed and put into his wife's milk on the morning she died." He turned to the solicitor. "Tasteless, I think you said they were?"

"Yes," agreed Latham. "Yes—according to Angela. Perhaps one should check with Craddock on that point, but Angela definitely told me she thought James had given them to the child in milk."

"In milk?" asked Masters. "Or with milk?"

Latham frowned. "Now you have asked me, I can't answer that. My impression is that Angela said he had been given milk and pills—there was a dirty glass to show it had been used. She said Robin must have awakened . . ."

"Or been awakened," said Green laconically.

". . . and wanted a drink. That's what makes me think the pills must have been in the liquid. I mean, if Robin had asked simply for a drink, might he not have made some objection to being given more pills? I know very little about small children, but I should imagine that persuading a child to take a large number of tablets, however small, would be an undertaking that could hardly be carried out in complete silence. And the mother was there, in the room. Asleep, admittedly, but surely with an ear attuned to pick up the slightest murmur from her sick child." Latham reddened, looked round his companions and finished lamely: "I understand that mothers are like that."

"They are, indeed," said Sir Francis gravely. "I think you have made an excellent deduction there, Latham."

"So do I," said Masters. "One I am fully prepared to accept."

"They always try the same trick the second time if they're not caught the first," said Green resignedly. "Tasteless and pale blue. Just the colour to not be seen in milk. A palmful in the glass to kill a sick child and the same amount to knock out a woman."

This summing up was undoubtedly a milestone in the investigation. Masters had been prepared to start by accepting the assurances of both March and Hill that Connal was guilty of murder. But he felt much happier now he had proved it to his own satisfaction. Proved it, true, without material proof. By speculation only, perhaps. But the jigsaw of coincidence and surmise was taking shape, each piece fitting so perfectly and so firmly that even now, though incomplete, it could be lifted and shaken without dislodging any of the bits so laboriously inserted.

Hill was not so happy. "You should have let me know all this, Mr Latham. You have been concealing a serious crime."

"What I have told you is hearsay, Mr Hill. Valueless in a court of law. Besides, it was a client-solicitor confidence. I could not volunteer the information while Angela was alive. Had I done so, would you have arrested Connal? Of course not. There was no proof. Nor could I speak of this after her death, except in special circumstances like tonight when I have been specifically asked to do so and we are talking very much off the record."

Hill accepted this with a grimace. Masters knew what was irking the local detective. Hill had patently failed to bring home the crime to Connal, but was now feeling that he would have been as successful as his former chief had he had the same information at his disposal. Hill, Masters thought regrettably, was forgetting that he had been in a position to cull all this information for himself, had he set about it in the right way; forgetting that the facts are always there, if properly elicited; forgetting that the good detective is the one with eyes to see and recognise facts, ears attuned to hear them, and the imagination to tell him where to look, when to listen and how to assemble the knowledge thus gained.

Masters turned to the solicitor. "Mr Latham, you've been of the greatest help. If it is any consolation to you, I can say that we all accept Mrs Connal's story—her impression—without reservation. We must now hope we can find some way to enable Sir Francis to pull our chestnuts out of the fire on Monday morning in the face of a judge who is unlikely to allow fresh witnesses to be called and a defence counsel who will, naturally, object strongly to the introduction of any fact or statement that has not been mentioned by earlier witnesses. Thank you, too, for your frankness in disclosing details of what must have been a very painful affair for you personally."

Sir Francis spoke up quickly. "I hope I don't need to tell you, Latham, that I shall not breathe one word of what you've told me. Your account has merely made stronger our determination to get our man. I hope your efforts will help Masters and the others to find me some effective way of doing it."

Latham got to his feet. "I wish you every success, Sir Francis. I don't think I'm a vindictive man, but I thought the world of Angela. . . ."

After Latham had left them, Masters asked: "I take it that all three of you have arrived at the same conclusion as I have?"

"That Connal is a pathological case?" asked Green, drily. "It sticks out a mile. He's as full of his own bloody froth and conceit as Wembley stadium is of spectators at a cup final. Nothing was going to stand in his way."

"Whilst agreeing with that substantially," said March, "I would also like it to be expressed in less general terms, Mr Green."

"His Nibs is the boyo to do that."

"How do you see it, George?"

"At its simplest? That his intention all along has been to have Dodson's Engineering for his own."

"Go on, Chief," said Hill. "There's little solid proof as yet, but your hypothesis has come good so far."

"I believe that even his small son must not be allowed to stand in Connal's way, because one day that small son would inherit the company and then Connal could be, in effect, his own son's employee. And that prospect didn't suit his book."

"But . . ." began Hill.

"Can it!" said Green. "Use your nous, matey. Latham gave the provisions of the will that had left all her father's loose cash and goods to Angela Connal, while the Dodson holdings were only to be hers, in trust, until the boy came of age. Then they were to go to him. So the lad would have become by far the largest shareholder and probably chairman, while his dad remained the under-strapper."

Hill nodded.

"But the lad died before his mother," went on Green. "So the shares she was holding in trust for him reverted to her by a provision of the will. That meant that as Connal had already got rid of his son, only his wife stood in the way of him laying his hands on the shares."

"But why murder a little boy?" demanded Hill. "So soon? Why not wait until he was grown up?"

"For reasons best known to Connal himself," replied Green. "But I've got my own ideas about it. First, it's easier to knock off a little chap than a hulking great brute of rising twenty-one. Second, it's easier to kill a kid who's sick than one who's well. Third, it's easy when there's dangerous medicine handy, kindly supplied by the doctor. Fourth, it makes it look like an accident if anybody ever suspects anything. Fifth, who's to know whether a boy that's ill when he's three is ever going to be ill again before he's sufficiently grown up to notice and resist a bit of hanky-panky like murder? And lastly, I reckon Connal wanted his boy dead soonest, for his own peace of mind and because he knew there would have to be a long gap between killing the boy and his mother, and he wanted to feel those shares in his hands as soon as ever he could."

The spelling out of this motive seemed to satisfy March. Hill was shaking his head, not in disagreement, but as if to indicate that he would never be able to achieve the creative styling of the solutions to problems that separated a man of the calibre of Masters from lesser lights in the profession. But at least—and at last—Hill had recovered his enthusiasm for what they were about.

"Come on, Chief, let's get him. Sew him up tight."

Masters smiled. "I think we've cleared away a lot of the dead wood. Enough, at any rate, to permit us to move on to the *modus operandi* of the fire-raising. And in this connection, I must say that the report from the Chief Fire Officer is not as full as I would have expected."

"I thought it was pretty good myself, Chief."

"I get the impression he only included what he thought would be pertinent to your case. I want to see the notes he—and others—made on the site."

"Tonight, George?"

"No, Frank. Tomorrow morning. Bill Green and I are going to have a quick drink and then we are heading for home. We'll be back here at ten in the morning."

CHAPTER VI

As MASTERS DROVE his own Jaguar towards London, Green——who for once had forsaken the back seat in which he preferred to travel and so was beside Masters—asked: "Why the fire report, George? We don't know much about arson and suchlike and we haven't much time to go into it thoroughly."

Masters, who guessed that Green had consented to sit tightly strapped into the front passenger seat because, at this hour of the night, the traffic was thinner, was driving quite slowly in order not to further frighten his assistant.

"I suppose I'm clutching at straws, Bill. I didn't say so back there in the hotel, but we haven't nailed Connal yet. We've got a lot of circumstance—motive and all the rest of it—and we know how he planned everything. But planning takes place in the mind. It leaves no material clues for the likes of us to pick up and exhibit in court except by the lengthy process of eliciting a hint here, a nuance there and, in general, by making use of every witness, and building up a reasonable picture thereby."

"I know," said Green. "The witnesses are all gone, so Sir Frank has no foundation on which to build. Connal has had his say and made a good impression. The prosecution can't—won't be allowed to—introduce anything of what we now know."

"If Frank were as much as to mention anything of what we've deduced today, Connal would only have to deny it and it would make our case worse with the jury who would simply regard it as a last desperate attack of unauthenticated sniping by the prosecution that had failed to prove its case."

Green grunted and started to hunt for his cigarettes, the seat belt restricting the search. "I'm like a tinned earwig," he growled. "Trussed up like an oven-ready guinea fowl."

Masters explained how—with gentle movement on the part of the wearer—the seat belt would give sufficiently to allow reasonable freedom. Green followed instructions and was soon puffing away. "So you reckon . . . what, George?"

"It's going to be a game of snap," replied Masters. "Frank has to slap a card in and make his point before Cuddles or Connal know what's hit them."

"What you're saying is that we've got to find just one question—because that's all we'll be allowed to fire off—just one question the answer to which will reverse everything that has gone on so far."

"More or less."

"Impossible."

"How else can we manage it?"

"God knows, and He won't split."

"Exactly."

"We don't 'arf pick 'em," grumbled Green. "As nasty a case of double murder as it's been our misfortune to run across in a month of Sundays, and as easy as kiss-your-hand to investigate and solve, and we can't even get the case heard in court. It makes you want to puke, George."

"It does," agreed Masters quietly.

Green looked across at him. "I know how it's affecting you, chum. You've got a small son and a bonny wife . . ."

"I feel almost as if Connal had done it to them," grated Masters. "When I think of that little chap . . ."

"Cut it out," said Green sharply. "Forget it until tomorrow. Then we'll do what we can. Though come to think of it, if he gets away with murdering his missus, couldn't we charge him with killing the child?"

"The thought had occurred to me, Bill, but I think not. It took place some years ago and the trail is cold. Besides, we couldn't prove it without mentioning the murder of Mrs Connal, and we most definitely wouldn't be allowed to drag that up again, once Connal had been cleared."

"You're right, worse luck. And we've always got to remember that juries don't like convicting in cases that are years old, anyway, so we might as well save our breath to cool our porridge. But we're still left with a hell of a problem."

"We are, indeed. That is why we now have to turn to the actual murder itself. To the act of preparing and setting fire to the house. I have no means of knowing if what the C.F.O. noted at the time will help, but it was obvious from the transcript that Frank was not given any really hard facts to use. Not positive ones at any rate. Only negatives, such as the statement that neither petrol nor paraffin was used. What good is that?"

"None. But a specialist bloke appearing in court is not asked to make guesses. He can only say what he knows is true and what he can substantiate, no matter what his private opinions may be."

"Right. But I want those opinions. They could spark us off on some track."

"And if they don't?"

"They've got to."

"Then what?"

"Then we've got to hit upon some pertinent question which will either rock Connal back on his heels or which will appeal to Judge Cleghorn as being so relevant that he will allow Frank to pursue the point."

"Despite any objection from Cudlip?"

"Yes."

"The best of British, chum."

"Thanks."

"And there's one other thing to pray for."

"I know. A hung jury. To be honest that's what I'm aiming for, Bill. If we could plant just enough doubt in some of their minds . . . so that they wouldn't agree."

"I know. A re-trial and you're home and in the dry. But to aim for a hung jury . . . well, I've never known a Jack, or any other cop, go for that."

"Neither have I. But it's an indication of how desperate I reckon our position to be."

"What we need," said Green, flicking his cigarette stub out of the window, "is a good night's sleep. We can't think straight after a fourteen-hour day."

Masters drove on steadily in the direction of Green's house. "I'll pick you up at nine, Bill."

"I shan't mind if it's a quarter past—being Sunday."

"No, I suppose not."

Green turned sharply. "What does that mean?"

"What?"

"Oh, come on! You've got some idea."

"Nothing, I assure you, except . . ."

"Ah!"

"I was going to say a bit of reading."

"Oh, aye! What sort of reading?"

"I was wondering whether any of the pundits have ever before found themselves in our position, and if so, how they have coped with it."

"Leave it, chum. Our pal Connal is a nutcase. A big-headed slob, and I can't see that anything we can do now is going to crack him."

"George!" Wanda came forward to greet him.

"Darling, you should be in bed and asleep."

"I watched the chat show. It hasn't been over all that long."

Masters kissed her.

"The young man?"

"I fed him at ten. Keep your fingers crossed that he'll go through till six."

Wanda moved across to the wine cupboard. "Whisky?"

"I'd prefer coffee. Black, please."

She turned. "Oh, no! That means you want to stay awake."

"For ten minutes or so. To look something up."

"George, you really are the world's worst. Come through to the kitchen with me and talk while I make the drinks."

Wanda listened carefully as her husband recounted the gist of what had been said and deduced during the day. By the time he had finished, he was starting on his second cup of black coffee.

"That little boy, George! And the wife . . ."

Masters nodded.

"You've got emotionally involved."

"How could I help but feel it?"

"You mustn't. He's mad! A psychotic!"

"Bill called him a nutcase that I couldn't crack."

"Bill's right."

"Thanks."

"About him being a nutcase, I mean. But not about you not being able to convict him. But . . ."

"Mm?"

"You said you were going to read up some former cases to see if you could get a hint as to how to proceed: to see if there was some precedent, presumably, for getting the trial stopped or new evidence introduced. Right?"

"It's a faint hope, but I ought to try it."

"If you want my advice you'll forget precedents and concentrate on Connal's weaknesses. You say he's some sort of psychotic, so why not. . . ?"

Masters smothered a yawn.

"Darling!"

"Sorry, Wanda. I'll do as you suggest. I'll be upstairs in a few minutes. Those books that doctor gave me after we caught the schizophrenic who laid out his victims in the form of a cross. They deal with psychotics. A chapter to each major type. I'll read . . ."

She laid a hand on his sleeve. "I don't want to stop you. There's a lot more coffee in the percolator. Rinse your cup under the cold tap before you come up. And don't wake your elder, unmarried son."

"Elder? I've only got one and I've only had him for a few months."

She smiled at him. "You never know your luck."

"No forensic report?" asked Green when they arrived at the hotel next morning.

"No," replied Hill. "It wasn't considered necessary. The body was virtually burned away—charred beyond recognition and only bones left. It was accepted that she had died in the fire."

"We're not saying she didn't. But examination of the site of the fire? Forensic should have had a look at that."

"It was left to the Chief Fire Officer. He's our local expert."

Green grunted in disgust. March said: "It looked easy at the outset, Mr Green. Inspector Hill got it right. It is just the unexpected character of the accused that has thrown us. I must admit I've never encountered so plausible a rogue as Connal."

"Are you saying," asked Hill, "that despite everything, we may not be able to nail him?"

Masters, who had brought a briefcase with him and had been consulting some of the papers it contained, looked up and said: "There's a distinct possibility he will get away with it."

Hill was dismayed.

"Oh, and by the way, I'm expecting D.S. Reed to come out with some material for me later. You'll be able to give him lunch, Frank?"

"Nothing easier. When you say material. . . ?"

"Papers, books, that sort of thing."

"References," grunted Green. "You sat up late reading till all hours after all," he accused.

"For barely twenty minutes. Wanda agreed with you, Bill, and made me cut it short. So I read one of those cribs I was given years ago, and it mentioned further reading references. Reed is getting them for me."

"I always said Wanda had more sense than you."

Masters grinned. "Now, Hill, what about the C.F.O.'s notes?"

"Here they are, Chief. He's lent us his pocket-book. He's a bit worried about the turn things have taken. Wondering whether he missed something."

"Does 'em good to keep 'em on their toes," said Green.

Masters read for a moment or two. Then he remarked: "The C.F.O. suggests that electrical wires could have been bared to cause simultaneous shorts in the vicinity of the inflammable material." He looked up. "Who is enough of an electrician to tell me what that means?"

Hill shrugged. March said: "I would take that to mean that the wires produced a spark."

Green shook his head. "No good," he said. "If those wires shorted out, the fuses would blow, and there'd be no more sparks to come. I know if I wanted to start a dirty great fire I'd make sure I was going to succeed and not trust to one spark."

"Wouldn't it depend on the material he wished to ignite? After all, the old flint and tinder . . ."

"That's not my point, Sir Frank. Everybody knows Murphy's Law, where a single spark made by mistake will certainly set fire to a house. But by the same law, if you want to set fire to a house, one spark will definitely not do it. Connal isn't the sort of bloke to have trusted one spark."

"I think you're both right," said Masters. "Bill must be on safe ground when he says some more prolonged method of fire-raising was used. But you, Frank, could have a point when you say it would depend on the material he wished to ignite. Unfortunately, the C.F.O. does not suggest what that material could have been, so we must speculate again."

Hill shook his head slowly. "I'd like some material evidence, Chief. It's vital."

"Don't get impatient, Hill," said March. "The Chief Super is doing famously."

"Help me through this," requested Masters. "Connal would use the least bulky of highly inflammable materials, wouldn't he? By that, I mean he wouldn't be likely to instal bales of straw, for instance."

"Getting them into the house unseen would have been difficult."

"The official report says there was no evidence of paraffin or petrol having been used," said Hill. "Evidently they leave traces that can easily be picked up. A lead residue, I think."

"Right," said Masters. "So what would he use, bearing in mind that we think whatever it was had only small bulk?"

"Come on," growled Green. "Tell us. I bet you looked it all up last night."

"I confess I did. I think the answer is benzine. According to the books it is a highly inflammable, volatile liquid that can be bought readily from any store or chemist in small containers as a cleansing fluid or obtained easily enough in industry as a commercial solvent. It is a petroleum ether and, in its pure state, leaves no residue after burning."

"Untraceable?" asked Green.

"Apparently—in both senses. Untraceable after a fire, and if commonly used in industry, almost certainly available at Dodson's by the gallon."

"That sounds more like it," agreed Hill, "but the C.F.O.'s investigations found no tins or bottles the benzine could have been in."

"Of course not, laddie," said Green. "They'd be ditched somewhere along the road to Birmingham."

"Right," said Masters. "He took them out of the house in his briefcase. But that is unimportant. Benzine is highly volatile, so it evaporates quickly, and it is the vapour that is highly inflammable. Remembering that the sites of the fires were in three relatively small cupboards . . ." Masters looked across at Hill, encouraging the local man to join in what could be developing into a brainstorming session.

"Got it, Chief. He put them there on purpose to get an atmosphere laden with vapour so that when a spark came—whoosh! The whole lot went up like . . . like . . . ."

"Except there wasn't a spark," grated Green.

"Spark, flame, source of heat— whatever it was," said Hill.

"So, ideally", said March, joining in eagerly, "he would want some open vessel like a bowl that would give the liquid a large surface area to facilitate the evaporation."

"Quite right, Frank," said Masters. "The airing cupboard particularly, with its higher temperature, would draw the vapour off at a merry rate. But he didn't use earthenware bowls, otherwise they would have been found after the fire—or bits of them."

"Among all that much?" queried Green. "In a house like that there'd be china and crockery all over the place. The bits and pieces of three bowls would have no significance."

"Agreed, Bill. But you yourself said that a bloke like Connal would leave nothing to chance. I know you were talking about electric fuses, but when houses burn, they often leave funny remains. You know what I mean. Something like one wall left standing with bits of each floor left jutting out with the remains of beds and wardrobes left teetering. . . ."

"You're right," agreed Green. "He'd not want anything that could survive, even by chance. So no ovenware bowls."

"Plastic, perhaps," suggested Hill.

"No go, lad," retorted Green. "Not all plastic burns. Look at the trouble the local incinerators have with all those plastic cups. You can't get a decent ash-dump these days that doesn't look as if it had been in a snowstorm."

Masters agreed. "My guess is he used wooden bowls. You can buy them anywhere. And they would burn right away in a hot fire—their ashes indistinguishable from those of the teak sideboard, oak dressing table or mahogany piano case."

"Now that *is* a possible fact," said Hill eagerly.

"Only if you make it so," said Masters.

"That's right, lad. Get your troops out. They've got to knock up the owner of every shop for miles around that sells wooden bowls. Interview owners and assistants. You've got less than twenty-four hours before the trial restarts tomorrow."

"But, Chief . . ." protested Hill, "there could have been wooden bowls in the house."

"Very likely, but Connal wouldn't have used them."

"No?"

"In a house like Ashbury House, the bowls would be used for some specific purpose—like holding fruit. Connal had to make his preparations in advance, knowing that his wife could walk around her house and go into any room. Housewives notice things. If she saw a heap of pears, apples and grapes on her sideboard, Mrs Connal would want to know . . ."

"But he wouldn't have to leave the fruit there, Chief. He could have disposed of it."

"She'd still have noticed," asserted Green. "A bloody great space where a bowl of fruit should have been? And even if she wouldn't have noticed, our boyo couldn't have afforded to take the risk. Don't forget that the neighbour—Mary Brignell—said in evidence that Connal had asked his wife not to get up to see him off that morning. And then Mrs Connal's reported reply, 'You've been moving about the house for ages'. It adds up. He had to move about setting up his stuff. He knew his wife was a rotten sleeper.

There was every chance she'd get up—as she did. And once she was up there was every chance she'd notice if something had been changed about the house. That's why his choice of sites for the fires was clever—besides the fact of them being small rooms that would fill with vapour. I don't suppose many women go straight to the cupboard under the stairs or into the loft when they get up."

"She might go to the airing cupboard for clean underwear."

"Not birds like this Connal dame. They have it all in drawers. But even if she did want something special like a hot bath-sheet, if her airing cupboard was anything like any I've ever seen, it would be easy enough to hide a bowl of benzine round the back of the tank or under a lot of the stuff that hangs down."

"That's right enough," agreed March. "And even if it isn't, Mr Hill, it's a chance we can't afford to overlook. We must try everything."

"I'm on my way," said Hill. "Everybody available will be going round those shopkeepers inside ten minutes."

"Good."

Hill left them to give his instructions. Green sighed with relief when the door had closed behind him. "I don't know what's up with the lad. Anybody would think we weren't trying to help him. He never used to be like that when he was a sergeant."

"I can understand him," said March, offering Green a cigarette. "He knows he can never work like you two. Any success he has will come from following the book. So he does that. But the book has let him down this time. He reckons he's failed, and that hurts. Particularly when you two come in and show him how and where, but too late—in his opinion—to do him any good. Would you be enthusiastic in those circumstances? To know you've got a particularly nasty murderer in your hands, but you've got to let him go because you haven't got him in the right grip?"

"By the short and curlies?"

"Quite. And then to further dampen down his optimism, almost the first words George uttered this morning were to say that he considered there was a distinct possibility that Connal would get away with it. Our friend Hill must feel as if he were swimming in treacle."

Green seemed unimpressed by these words. "Whilst agreeing with you, Sir Frank," he said, "you must see that it would be wrong for His Nibs here to build up the expectations until he is sure we can win. I thought we'd brought up young Hill better than that."

"He's been his own boss—virtually—for a year or two now," said Masters. "In the old days he was under our direction. He'll have changed, or been changed."

Green grunted to show both that he appreciated the point and to deplore what he considered lesser standards outside his own sphere of influence. "What about the rest of those notes, George?"

"Give me a moment or two to read on a bit."

"I'll get coffee sent up," said March.

The coffee had arrived and had been poured out before Masters looked up. "I knew it!"

"What?"

"Frank, you should have insisted on Hill seeing these notes. He shouldn't have been allowed to rely solely on the C.F.O.'s official report."

"Don't blame me, George. How did I know he hadn't seen the notes? I use the material I'm given. Anyhow, what have you found?"

"Listed among the destroyed but still recognisable objects found in the rubble is a typewriter. The name was still decipherable. An Ajax Superb 23. Hill is supposed to have searched everywhere for the typewriter that produced the anonymous letter. He tried all the Dodson's office machines. . . ."

"Of course he did, in case an employee was getting at Connal. But don't forget the idea that Connal sent that letter himself never entered our heads until you put it there yesterday. So Hill wouldn't search the Ashbury House rubble, would he?"

The door opened at that moment and Hill entered. "Did I hear my name being taken in vain?"

"You did," said March. "Mr Masters says there was a type-writer found in the rubble of Ashbury House."

"I expect there was. Connal admitted in court to owning one."

"What typeface was the anonymous letter written in?" asked Masters.

"My note on the subject says twelve-point Calansca," said March.

"Twelve-point is the commonest face there is."

"This wasn't common," said Hill. "It looked funny."

"How?" demanded Green.

"There was something different about it. The lettering looked thin and . . . how can I put it? . . . widespaced."

"I'd say from memory," added March, "that it was clear cut."

"That's it," agreed Hill. "But look here, Chief, we won't be able to test that machine in the rubble. Those typemetal characters are very soft. They'll have completely melted away."

"All the same," said Masters, "I'd like to have the registered number of the machine. If we could trace it back and find it was one that had been fitted with twelve-point Calansca characters . . ."

"On a Sunday?" queried Green.

"Before ten-thirty tomorrow morning."

"Leave it to me, Chief," said Hill. "It's just the registered number you want? The one stamped on the chassis?"

"If somebody hasn't whipped it," said Green.

"C.F.O. Mailer collected all the bits and pieces together. They're in plastic bags in the garage. Locked up."

"In that case . . ." Green got to his feet. "I'll come with you. I'd like a run out before my Sunday roast and Yorkshire pud."

Shortly after Green and Hill had left, Detective Sergeant Reed arrived with a number of photocopied documents for Masters.

"All there?"

"All here, Chief. At least all we could lay hands on before the R.S.M. library opens tomorrow."

"Thank you. Would you like to go off for a coffee break now, while I read these? Come back in about half an hour."

"Right, Chief."

"Something of interest?" asked March when Reed had gone.

"I hope so. Look, Frank, it will take me at least twenty minutes to digest this lot. Would you mind if. . . ?"

"Not in the least, my dear chap. I haven't had a chance to open my Sunday paper yet and I like to take my time over browsing through it."

"Excellent. We'll both have a reading period."

There was virtual silence in the room for the next half hour or so. When Reed returned, Masters was pencilling attention marks in the margins of the papers opposite bits he obviously considered important.

"Come in, Reed. I've nearly finished."

Reed took a chair without speaking. At last Masters looked up. "Fine. Everything I want is here. You can go back now, if you want to, or you can stay here for lunch. Sir Francis has invited you."

"I'll stay, sir. I'd like to hear what it's all about." Reed turned to the Q.C. "Thanks for the invitation to lunch, sir."

March lowered his paper and peered over his reading glasses at the sergeant. "Pleasure, Reed. Interested in cricket?"

"The only chance I get to watch it these days is on Sunday afternoons sometimes, on the telly. The limited overs games."

"Me, too. I get quite angry when the matches are rained off. I was looking forward, a fortnight ago, to that last Somerset and Essex game of the season, when damn me it was washed out and there wasn't a cloud in the sky in my corner of the world. Why on earth . . ."

"May I butt in?" asked Masters.

"Of course, George. Sorry."

"We've got a lot of work still to do."

"Yes. I was just thinking, I'll have most of mine to do late tonight, because though you've reconstructed the crime admirably, it still isn't finished, is it?"

"No."

"And I'm still not sure I'm going to pull it off in court."

"Why not, Sir Francis?" asked Reed and then apologised. "Sorry, sir, I shouldn't have asked."

"Of course you should ask. I'll tell you why not. It's too late on in the trial. We're at the end. Connal, the accused, is in the box, and he's the last—as the accused usually is. The defence has no more witnesses for me to question, and all mine are gone. How am I going to prove the Chief Superintendent's reconstruction of the crime without witnesses from whom to elicit the facts?"

"Can't you ask to call new witnesses or recall old ones, sir?"

"Not at this stage. At least, I can try, but Mr Justice Cleghorn is not the sort to agree very readily to that sort of ploy, and Cudlip would oppose it strongly—as he would have every right to do."

"Sir, couldn't you rattle the accused if you now know everything that happened? Probably, if the judge could see the accused was rattled, he'd accede to your request to call fresh evidence."

March said: "It won't be too easy to upset Connal. He's a bumptious character."

Masters joined in. "That could mean, Reed, that he's all the more likely to be deflated by a bit of daft questioning. At least that is what Sir Francis and I are hoping for. Just one dirty great question with which to confound him."

"Or several if we can manage to get them in without objections being raised," added March.

"And you think that will do it?" asked Reed, sceptically.

"That's the only way open to us, Sergeant. We're not saying we're sure about it. I want to bring back Latham, the solicitor, and the milkman and the family doctor."

"In fact," said Masters, "Sir Francis would like to start the trial all over again."

"Precisely. That's what I'd like. To start afresh."

"Too late, Frank. So you'll just have to lead off with a totally unexpected question which shows you've rumbled him, and the answer to which can be checked by facts. Play it off the cuff after that, but never let up. You can keep Connal there as long as you like, put what questions you like as long as they're relevant, make insinuations from inside knowledge. Get the jury to appreciate that you know a lot more than has been brought out, and prepare them for hearing a reasonable hypothesis from you when you address them. But you don't need me to tell you. Connal's reaction will dictate your line to some extent. You've done it scores of times."

"Maybe. But I'd still like a chance to recall certain people.

However, I'll play it your way and see how it turns out."

"Once you get into court, you'll find it will come sweet. Listen . . ." Masters leaned across the table and spoke in a quiet voice for the next ten minutes or so, only interrupting the flow to bring to the attention of Sir Francis the points he had marked in the papers as each bit became relevant. He had scarcely finished before there was a knock on the door, and Green and Hill entered, the latter carrying a transparent polythene bag by the neck.

"Success?"

"Yes, Chief."

"Excellent. That seems to be a good cue for a drink. Can it wait if we were to go down to the bar for a quickie before lunch?"

"And how!" grunted Green. "Give us a minute. I'd like to use Sir Frank's handbasin. That stuff was mucky."

"In that case, we'll line one up for you."

"Could I ask you to avoid discussing this business downstairs?" asked March. "The defence knows that we are in conclave, but I think it is vital that no word of exactly what we are doing should leak out, and there are spies about."

"Nice pub, this," said Green as he and Hill joined the others at the bar and found a tankard of beer already drawn for him. He took a long and noisy gulp.

"You'll probably change your mind when you've seen the menu," said Masters, passing him the card.

"Family Sunday Lunch!" exclaimed Green. "Duckling, and no choice? No roast beef and Yorkshire pud? No wonder this country's going downhill. Everybody eats cereal for breakfast and thinks that a bit of duck with a slice of orange stuck on it is the be-all of eating." He took another noisy gulp of beer and then added: "And no rice pud, either. Only compost of pears."

"Compote," said Hill.

"Compost I said, lad, and compost I mean. Who's getting the next one in? I've nearly finished this one."

"We brought the remnants of the machine itself, Chief," said Hill. "But I'll not get it out unless you actually want to see it because it's filthy."

"All I want is the number."

"I've got it written down for you." He handed over a slip of paper. On it was written 189/69/AS23/ss. "Does that convey anything to you, Chief?"

"No mention of the typeface? No c for Calansca, for instance?"

"Nothing but what's there. AS23—that would be Ajax Superb 23, I suppose."

"Sixty-nine could be the year of manufacture," said March. "If so, one-eight-nine could be the machine number of that year."

"So if the typeface is included," said Green, "it must be denoted by the ss."

"ss!" said Masters. "This Calansca typeface—you said it was clean cut and thin. Could it be *sans serif*?"

"Come again, Chief?"

"I'm no expert on typography, either," confessed March. "What is *sans serif*?"

"It means lettering with all the little feet and ticks at the top cut off. All the cross bits. You must know what I mean. If *you* print a little L, you just draw a vertical straight line—that's *sans serif*. The normal typewriter, however, gives the L a little foot at the bottom and a tick at the top. . . ."

"Don't go on, George. That's it. The letter itself was put into court as an exhibit, so you can't examine it."

"But that's how it was," agreed Hill. "I could perhaps get a photocopy tomorrow morning before the court opens, Chief."

"Don't bother." Masters turned to March. "It's not the best of tangible evidence, Frank, but we'll get a photograph of that number for you. I'm sure you can play about with it verbally. All the bit about *sans serif* and how coincidental it is that Connal should own a machine with so unusual a typeface and that his wife should receive a letter printed in that face. Got it?"

"It gels," growled Green.

"Leave it to me," said March, making a note.

"And something else, Frank."

"Yes?"

"Remember that in his evidence, Latham stressed that the letter filled Mrs Connal with an unidentifiable fear? Make this point.

Stress it. She knew—subconsciously—that it came from her husband. Subliminally she recognised it from years back and her subconscious told her to beware—that there was more to that letter than just a sneaky bit of gossip."

"I like it," said Green.

"That's all very well, but it's not material fact," said Hill.

"But it's logical," said Green. "And Cudlip can't stop Sir Francis introducing that line, because Connal is the only witness who could be questioned about his own typewriter. He's the only one still alive who knew it was there. The judge will allow it."

Hill was mollified by Green's explanation and further cheered by March, who said: "It may not be material fact, Mr Hill, but it is the keystone to the whole puzzle. It fits exactly, and that tells us without any doubt, that the Chief Superintendent's solution is correct in every detail. With what we know now, and a fresh start to the trial, we could send Connal down without a shadow of doubt. As things are—well, I'm getting useful bits and pieces to play with."

"And," said Green quietly, "I can give you a few more. Three to be exact."

Masters grinned. "You've been gainfully employed, Bill? I thought you had. You were in such good form in the bar and at table."

Green got up and went to the polythene bag Hill had carried in. From it he drew a small white bundle.

"I had to use my nuffer to wrap these in," he said as he laid the handkerchief on the table and carefully opened it up.

There was a moment of silence as all five men gazed at the contents.

"Yes," breathed Masters with satisfaction.

Reed, who was not in the picture as the others were, asked: "What the hell? They're bits of an element from an electric fire."

March said: "You'd better explain fully, Mr Green. As to an idiot child, please, because I shall have to have it all very clearly in my own mind if I'm to explain to a jury exactly what we are suggesting."

"Go ahead, Bill," said Masters. "Everything about them. But

133

before you do, can I just say that I reckon Hill owes you more than a drink for this."

"A barrel?" suggested Green with a grin, delighted by Masters' reception of his find.

"Hold it, hold it," said Hill. "We haven't heard yet what's the importance of these bits of wire."

"So I'll tell you," said Green. "Mailer's boys obviously did a good job on that site. They combed it. The garage has all the bits of metal they could find from taps to door knobs, with an oven and a fridge and all the rest thrown in. And they've laid it out—all the big bits separately and all the odds and ends in a heap. I turned the heap over while Hill got the typewriter. I found one of these bits first. I had to dig for the others.

"You'll see that each end of each length has been looped. Note this, Sir Frank, because I think it's significant. I reckon Connal bought a new element for an electric fire, and he snipped it into three—one bit for each cupboard. Then I guess he put all three pieces into the same circuit. But he didn't solder them in, because solder has a low melting point and would run off as soon as the elements got hot, but before they got hot enough to ignite anything. And once one blob of solder had gone, the circuit would go dead. But these elements, which go brittle with use, are much more pliable when new. So he could loop the ends and actually tie in the cable to make sure nothing came adrift."

"How do we know that?" asked Hill.

"We don't," retorted Green. "But can you suggest any reason why three bits of electric element should have their ends looped, unless it was for the purpose I've described? If it had been an element from an electric fire that was ruined in the fire, the element could have broken into three—but the ends would be clean breaks, not bloody loops."

"The D.C.I. is right," said Masters. "No elements are looped normally, or if they are, they are simply turned to go under a washer which, when tightened by a screw, holds them in place." He turned to Green. "There should have been wires attached."

"Not necessarily, Chief," said Reed. "Soft copper wire would melt in a hot fire, where the elements, which are made to stand heat, would not."

"You're sure of that?"

"Rag-and-bone men recover old copper wire by burning the rubber coating off, Chief. But they don't use a furnace. More of a cooler, smoky sort of fire, so as not to melt the core. But even so, they often pick up blobs of copper after the fire's cold."

"Thanks. So the D.C.I. has given us the method. Now, Hill, it's up to your lads to find those bowls."

"It'll be like looking for a needle in a haystack. He could have bought them anywhere. And then we've got to find the assistant who remembers Connal. . . ."

Masters snapped his fingers.

"Where's Mrs King? The housekeeper."

"She's living with her sister."

"In Elmhurst?"

"Yes. Twenty-three Barstow Street."

"Where's that?"

"About a mile from here."

"Right, come on. I want to see her."

"What about, Chief?"

"I want to know, dammit, if Connal was in the habit of paying cash or of shopping with a credit card."

"I can tell you that. He used a card."

"How do you know?"

"Because we took them off him when we arrested him."

"Right. Who gets his mail now? Since he was remanded in custody?"

"How do you mean, Chief?"

"Who paid his last credit card account? They come in monthly, don't they?"

"You're right, George!" shouted March. "By jove, you're right! Credit card accounts name the shops at which purchases are made, and the shops must keep invoices."

The light dawned on Hill. "Connal's solicitor has power of attorney because there are so many business matters."

"Latham?"

"No. After Latham gave him the boot, he went to Young."

Masters turned to Sir Francis. "Can we get that account from Young?"

"If he has it, I can get the court to order it to be produced. But I'd rather ask for it first. Give him the chance to co-operate before wheeling up the heavy artillery."

"You and Hill, between you?"

"If he's available this afternoon."

"It's worth a try," said Hill. "I'm ready when you are, Sir Francis." He turned to Masters. "And if Young won't play, Chief, I'm certain the credit people will in a case like this. They rely too heavily on us to sort out the backsliders to refuse co-operation."

CHAPTER VII

"SIR FRANCIS," said the judge, "when the court adjourned on Friday evening, you were about to cross-examine the accused. Are you ready to proceed now?"

"Certainly, m'lud."

"Before we begin . . . you hinted that you estimate your examination will take something like an hour?"

"I cannot, of course, m'lud, be precise."

"Quite. But the Court has to be administered, Sir Francis. Estimates of timings help my clerk and the administrator in their task."

Crown counsel bowed to indicate that he appreciated the point made by the bench. "I shall try to be economical with your time, m'lud."

Cleghorn glared, as if to show he found the reply less than felicitous, but Sir Francis had already started to busy himself with his papers and so the unspoken rebuke was lost on him.

"James Connal."

Cudlip half rose as the prisoner was moved from the dock to the witness box. It was an unconscious gesture from a kindly man— almost a solicitous greeting to his client. Connal appeared not to notice, but walked firmly between the two boxes. Green, sitting with Masters immediately behind crown counsel, whispered: "Cocksure bastard. He reckons he's got away with it all right."

Masters nodded. They had all worked until after ten the night before. He and Green had been back in Elmhurst before eight this morning to put the final touches to their part of the agreed scheme. March had spent long hours preparing his cross-examination, carefully schooled by Masters. Now the time had come to see just how successful the hard work of the weekend would be. Masters was too keyed-up to reply verbally to Green who seemed to realise this and, after making his comment about Connal, fell silent.

Green, normally an insensitive man, was, in fact, picking up something of the atmosphere of the court. He didn't know it, but the feeling in the courtroom was different from that on any of the preceding days of the trial. So far, not a word had passed between counsel and accused, but something akin to excitement—in himself, in Masters, March, Hill, Berger, Reed and the local constables who had helped them—seemed to be electrifying the environment. As yet, it didn't appear to have got through to Cudlip or Connal. The charge seemed to be locked up, as in a laser, ready to hurtle across space when the countdown should be made. So far the preliminaries were only proceeding as part of the build-up.

"Kindly remember," said the judge to Connal, "that you are still on oath."

"Yes, m'lud."

Connal looked sleek. His expensive suit sat easily on his figure. The striped shirt had been laundered and gophered so well that the collar shone. The club tie was impeccable. The gingery hair waved gently, and the well-barbered cheeks were glossy and healthily coloured. There was no prison pallor about James Connal. He stood erect in the dock, supporting himself with his arms, well-manicured fingers lightly curled round the top rim of the woodwork. He was, it seemed, confident and ready for anything.

March rose slowly to question him: peered at him closely for several seconds as though in the hope of intimidating him. When that appeared to fail, counsel had recourse to words.

"James Connal, you told the court on Friday that you own a typewriter."

"I certainly did own one. But I hadn't used it for years."

"It was still in your possession at the time of the fire which destroyed your home?"

"As far as I know, it was. I hadn't sold it or given it away, though my wife could well have done so. She was insistent on getting rid of any article for which we no longer had any apparent or regular use."

"Did she ever say she had disposed of it?"

"No."

"Would you please tell me the make of the machine?"

"The make? I'm not sure. As I said, I hadn't seen it for years."

"Did Mrs Connal possess a typewriter?"

"No."

"Nor your housekeeper, Mrs King?"

"No."

"Then we are at liberty to assume," said Sir Francis apparently off-handedly, but in as considered a way as a well-rehearsed leading actor at Stratford, "that the remains of any typewriter found in the rubble of Ashbury House would be those of your long-lost machine?"

"I suppose so."

"Do you mean yes?"

"Yes."

"Thank you."

March half-turned towards the judge. "M'lud, I now wish to produce the remains of a typewriter found in the ruins of the burned-out house."

One of Hill's detective constables carried the exhibit into the court on a tin tray and deposited it on the clerk's table in front of the bench. As Cleghorn peered down at it, March continued.

"You will see that the fire has done serious damage to the machine."

"Don't let us understate the catastrophe, Sir Francis. The machine is ruined. In fact, it is no longer a typewriter, but a fire-blackened mass of twisted metal." The judge turned to the jury. "I have stressed this point, because though I am as yet unaware of the prosecution's line of argument, we—that is you and I—whilst keeping an open mind, should view with some scepticism any attempt to glean evidence from a material exhibit which has so plainly suffered to such a degree as to be almost unrecognisable." Cleghorn looked at March as if inviting him to regard the typewriter as inadmissible and to canter through whatever else he had to say so that the job of summing up could begin.

March, however, was not prepared to be side-tracked.

"The fire has melted away the characters, m'lud, so we certainly cannot test the typeface. But that is by the way. I should like to assure the court that this exhibit has been in police keeping—under lock and key—since its retrieval by the Chief Fire Officer who investigated the fire.

"The accused has accepted that any typewriter found on the premises would belong to him." March turned to Connal. "Let me see if I can refresh your memory as to the make. It is an Ajax Superb."

Connal was confident enough to smile. "I remember now. My typewriter was an Ajax Superb."

Cudlip was plainly uneasy. He knew March too well to suppose that there was no good—and damaging—reason for the production of the typewriter and the questions connected with it. He rose. "M'lud . . ."

"Yes, Mr Cudlip?"

"My learned colleague has produced an exhibit without substantiating it in any way. It should have been placed before the Court so that the Fire Officer concerned could have vouched for it. As it is, we have merely Counsel's word that this . . . this heap of scrap iron is, in fact, what he claims."

"M'lud . . ." March was on his feet again.

"One moment, Sir Francis." Cleghorn turned to the jury. "The defence has a valid point, but at the moment I cannot rule that the evidence is inadmissible because the accused himself has gone at least some way towards validating it. Should improper use be made by the Crown of his admissions concerning the typewriter, I shall intervene on behalf of the defence. I have already warned you not to set too much store by evidence gleaned from so distorted an object."

Cudlip again rose. "M'lud, as my learned colleague has already admitted that the characters are destroyed and, therefore, are unable to be tested . . ."

"Please don't labour the point, Mr Cudlip. I have already assured the court that I shall protect the interests of the defence."

The judge then addressed the prosecution counsel. "Sir Francis, where is your present line of questioning leading us?"

"If your Lordship will bear with me, I think it will soon become apparent."

"Let us hope so. Now, may we please proceed."

March inclined his head towards the bench and then turned once more towards Connal. "As your counsel seems anxious that I should not pursue the question of the typewriter at this point, let me turn to Elizabeth Leacholt—Miss or Mrs. You stated on Friday that you did not know her."

"I didn't."

"At one point you went so far as to say that you doubted whether this woman has ever existed. Is this still your view?"

"It is. I certainly knew nothing of her, and nobody has been able to trace her. It seemed logical to me to doubt her existence."

March looked up from his papers. "It will be a surprise to you, perhaps, to learn that the prosecution shares your doubts as to the existence of Elizabeth Leacholt, will it not?"

"A great surprise. So much has been said about her."

"Quite."

The judge intervened. "You do realise what you have just admitted, Sir Francis?"

"I am aware, m'lud, that I agreed with the accused in doubting that the woman Leacholt exists, or has ever existed."

"Yet with previous witnesses you have striven to stress the part she played in the events leading up to this trial."

"Quite so, m'lud. With a purpose. The prosecution wished to establish that even though the woman herself is a lie—if I may use the term—that lie has, nevertheless, influenced the case before the court."

"A spectre at the feast, wielding a baleful power analogous to that of a real human being?"

"Just so, m'lud."

"I see. What now?"

"M'lud, I should now like to show the court a police photograph of the registered number-plate of the typewriter on the table before you."

Cudlip rose to object to the photographs being produced.

"M'lud," complained March, "I had the photographs prepared simply to spare you and the members of the jury the dirty and distasteful task of peering at a small, inaccessible plate on the chassis of the typewriter. If my learned colleague would prefer me to hand the exhibit round . . ."

"Very thoughtful of you, Sir Francis. We will see the photographs. Should Mr Cudlip wish to do so he can compare them with the plate on the machine to confirm that they are a true record."

"Thank you, m'lud."

Photographs were handed to the judge and to each member of the jury. March himself handed one to Cudlip before again addressing the jury.

"Please keep the photographs in your hands for the next few minutes. You will see, quite clearly, that the registered number is 189/69/AS23/SS. The AS23 component refers to the type of machine—an Ajax Superb 23—the make which the accused agreed a short time ago was that of the machine he himself owned. The six-nine component denotes the year of manufacture—1969—which bears out the claim made by the accused that the machine was, indeed, bought some years ago. The next component, one-eight-nine, tells us the machine number of that year—the one hundred and eighty ninth to be made in 1969." March looked up as if to see whether the jury had fully understood his explanation so far. Satisfied that they had, he turned to the judge.

"At this point, m'lud, I should like you to re-examine the unsigned letter which has already been exhibited. The one purporting to inform Mrs Connal that her husband had taken a lover called Elizabeth Leacholt."

The letter was passed up to the bench.

"I should like to draw your attention to the typeface, m'lud. You will see that it is somewhat unusual. It is . . ."

"I know what it is, Sir Francis. It is *sans serif.*"

March inclined his head. "Quite, m'lud. *Sans serif.*"

The judge turned to the jury to explain to them the meaning of *sans serif* and that it was an uncommon type of character.

"Thank you, m'lud." March again addressed the jury. "Now, I

should like you to look at the photographs again. To the final component—two letters, ss. They denote the kind of typeface with which the machine was fitted, and they stand for *sans serif*."

Cudlip was on his feet, protesting. "M'lud! This is pure speculation. It is . . ."

"Please, Mr Cudlip! The prosecution indulged the accused on Friday. There must be a little give and take in these matters, particularly as I cannot see how you can object to the prosecution interpreting the registration plate of a typewriter for the benefit of the jury. That does not mean that I shall not look after the interests of the accused, but, so far, no question pertaining to this particular point has been put to him. Meanwhile, I should tell you that I find that what Sir Francis has just shown us to be relevant to the case. It is the conclusions he attempts to draw from these recent facts that will be important. Please continue, Sir Francis."

March turned to Connal.

"You have said that Elizabeth Leacholt has never existed in the flesh. Could she have been a figment of your imagination?"

"Mine?"

"Yours."

"Certainly not."

"Did you not type that letter yourself on that machine and send it to your wife?"

"Of course not. Why should I do such a thing? No sane man would tell his wife he was having an affair with another woman— particularly if he wasn't."

"Do you not think it strange that a letter about a non-existent woman, typed in a very rare typeface—exactly the same as the one on your machine—should be sent to your wife?" The advocate's voice rose to crescendo point as he finished the question.

"Yes."

Green whispered: "Sir Frank's hotting it up."

Masters nodded in reply. "Did you notice the bit about no sane man telling his wife?"

"I got it. Did March?"

Masters shrugged as prosecuting counsel continued.

"Yes, you say?"

"Yes."

"Thank you." March changed his tone. "Your wife had not seen that typeface for years, had she?"

"I can't answer that question."

Cudlip rose. "M'lud, the witness cannot answer on behalf of another person."

Cleghorn grimaced. "Rephrase, Sir Francis."

"Your wife had not seen anything that had been typed on your machine for years, had she?"

"I hadn't used the typewriter for many years."

"At last! So, I now put it to you, James Connal, that your wife was unduly frightened by that letter, not because of the trivial gossip it contained, but because she recognised—probably subliminally—the typeface in which it was printed, and the memory so disturbed her, because she could not account for her unease, that she immediately sought the support of her solicitor."

The judge leaned forward. "Was that a question, Sir Francis?"

"Indeed, m'lud."

"It occurred to me that you may have been under the mistaken impression that you were addressing the jury. Mr Cudlip, I shall instruct the accused not to attempt to answer what was certainly not a question, nor to comment on it."

"Doesn't matter," murmured Green. "He got the point across."

"Thank you, m'lud," said Cudlip.

The judge turned to the jury. "The suggestions just made by learned counsel may well remain in your minds. You may well feel that those suggestions provide satisfactory answers to several of the baffling problems in this case. Who was the woman Leacholt? Who wrote the anonymous letter that mentioned her name? Why was that letter in a *sans serif* typeface? Why did so vague and generally phrased a letter cause Mrs Angela Connal to take such precipitate action? But I must remind you that prosecuting counsel was speculating. He has proved none of these things, and so you must not accept his suggestions as proven truth, no matter how neat and tidy a solution they provide. I shall have more to say about this before you retire." Cleghorn then turned again to March. "Sir Francis, I shall not permit you to sow dragons' teeth in this way. You will ask questions and not make speeches that are full of innuendo liable to influence the jury and incapable of being refuted or even replied to by the witness. I have already stated that I shall protect the accused from such attacks, and I intend to fulfil my promise. I shall be less than pleased should you again try to bulldoze some hypothesis or any further unsubstantiated speculation into these proceedings. Do I make myself clear, Sir Francis?"

"Perfectly clear, m'lud."

"And that," whispered Masters to Green, "is that."

"You reckon we've had it?"

"No. Just the opposite. Old Cleggers is beginning to see daylight and it is hurting his eyes, so he's given Frank a roasting . . ." He was interrupted by the judge addressing defence counsel.

"You keep bobbing up and down, Mr Cudlip. Did you wish to say something?"

"M'lud, this recent allegation by prosecuting counsel has made it imperative that I should confer with my instructing solicitor and the accused."

"You are asking for a break?"

"If your Lordship would be so kind."

"Very well. In the circumstances, and in view of my recent remarks, I shall accede to your request. Ten minutes, Mr Cudlip. The court will reassemble at five minutes to twelve."

As Cudlip, his junior and their solicitor hurried across the courtroom, Masters leaned forward to talk to March.

"Well done, Frank."

"You think so?"

"I do."

"So do I," asserted Green. "You've got Cleghorn worried, otherwise he wouldn't have gunned for you."

"He was rather outspoken, wasn't he? I'm still smarting a bit."

"No need to feel bad," continued Green. "You've got everybody on the hop. Cuddles is nearly foaling a mackerel."

"He's what?"

"He's running around spare."

"Good."

Masters said: "This break is a godsend. You couldn't have stage-managed it better, Frank. Bill, make sure that Hill and Reed keep the exhibit safely under cover. Get them to set everything up immediately in front of Frank now."

"Instead of carting it in at the critical moment?"

"I think so. Make sure it will be in full view of the bench and the jury as well as the witness box. There'll be a strip of white sheeting covering it. See it is free to whip away when the time comes."

"That side of it's all laid on," said Green. "The boys have got it mounted on a base of hardboard. They had to have because we didn't know Cleghorn would decide to decamp for a cup of coffee, did we?" Green got to his feet. "I'll go and see the lads. I'll be able to have a fag outside, too. Would you like me to have one for you as well?"

After Green had gone, March asked: "How's Connal?"

"Still full of himself," replied Masters. "As Bill Green said, you've rattled his Lordship and defending counsel more than you've affected the accused. They haven't taken him down. They're conferring behind the witness box. I can't see the whole scene, but I get the impression Connal is still in command of himself."

"Reassuring Cuddles, perhaps."

"Would Cuddles ask him if any of the things you alleged were true?"

"I don't think he dare at this stage. He's over there thanking his lucky stars that Connal confessed to owning a typewriter last Friday, so it won't look to the jury as though there's been a cover-up in that area. But Cuddles will be warning him."

"What about?"

"Admitting to too much too easily, and he'll be telling him to stick to yes and no answers should I get on to money. Young, the solicitor, must have told Cuddles I asked to see Connal's credit card statement. After the typewriter business, Cuddles will think I'm going to pull another flanker."

"Such as? You didn't tell Young why you wanted to see the statement."

"*Suggestio falsi*," said March with a grin. "I gave the impression

146

I wanted to check whether Connal had been sending expensive presents to members of his harem. I said, quite openly, that if they did not allow me to check I could jump to my own conclusions and drop a strong hint to the jury that there was something discreditable hidden in the statement."

"And?"

"Young was very happy to show me everything. He thought I was clutching at a whole bale of straws in the hope of getting something to pin on Connal today. He saw my request for the statement as the last hope of counsel without a single concrete fact to help him. And he knew—he was sure he knew—there was nothing incriminating in that credit card statement. So he let me have it."

"Excellent." Masters looked at his watch. "Now, where are those lads? Cleghorn will be resuming in a couple of minutes."

"Coming in now, bearing the bag of tricks carefully shrouded and suitably surrounded to cut it off from the vulgar gaze."

"Good." Masters stood and moved round to the front of counsel's bench. "Stand in front of it, Mr Hill, please. And you, Reed. For as long as possible. I'd like to hide its presence from the opposition if we can."

"I've brought a couple of newspapers, Chief," said Reed. "I thought I could half open them and plonk them on top so that we could even hide the cloth."

"Good thinking," growled Green. "Open the pink 'un up so as it looks as if Sir Francis had spent the recess doing a bit of speculating on something other than the case. It'll impress the judge and make Connal think he's got nothing to worry about."

"He's surely beginning to feel a bit of pressure," said Hill.

"Not him. He's still as full of bounce as an egg is full of meat. Did you hear him say that no *sane* man would write that letter to his wife? His Nibs picked that one up like a sparrow does a crumb."

"Why should the Chief do that?"

"He used it as a yardstick to gauge how much of the Old Adam there was still left in Connal. He reckons that when a nutter starts claiming he's sane it's a good sign."

"What of? That his confidence is being worn down?"

"No lad. That it's still intact."

"So we're losing."

"Winning."

"How do you make that out?"

"The bigger they are, the harder they fall," said Green enigmatically as a voice rang out: "Everybody rise."

The judge resumed the bench and Connal was back in the witness box.

"I trust you now have your instructions, Mr Cudlip?"

"Yes, thank you, m'lud."

"Then can we please get on?" asked Cleghorn petulantly. "We have wasted a lot of valuable time."

Sir Francis rose.

"I should like the accused to see this credit card, m'lud."

"Very well."

It was carried across to the box. When it had been handed up to Connal, March asked: "Is that your property?"

"Yes."

"Did you ever lose it?"

"Not until the police took it from me after my arrest."

"Then I would be correct in assuming that this statement of your account from the credit card company is a true list of purchases made by you?"

"Really, Sir Francis, is all this necessary?" asked Cleghorn as the statement was passed to Connal.

"Necessary, m'lud . . . and vital."

"Very well." The judge turned to Connal. "Is that your statement?"

"Yes, m'lud."

"Is it correct?"

"I can see no mistakes, but obviously I would need time to check it to be absolutely sure."

"We can call it correct. Let me see the statement." Cleghorn held out his left hand while he made a note with his right hand. After examining it, he placed it alongside his book.

Meanwhile, March, waiting for the signal to continue, had used the break to remove the newspapers covering the exhibit in front of him.

"Carry on, Sir Francis."

It seemed to Masters that March visibly summoned up all his histrionic ability at this moment. The barrister began casually enough: "Mr Connal . . ." The words came out slowly. "Please tell me . . ." March nonchalantly fingered the corner of the piece of white sheeting, striving hard to give the impression that he was slightly at a loss as to what question to ask. "Please tell me . . . why you bought three wooden sugar bowls from Chapman's of Kingston four days before you set fire to your house."

March whipped the sheet away.

For a moment there was silence, then the tension broke. Cudlip leapt to his feet to protest. "M'lud . . ." The judge appeared not to hear him, nor to notice the hum of conversation in the court. He was staring, fascinated, at the three wooden bowls, each four inches in diameter, and each topped by a coiled length of electric element, the three pieces of which had been wired together in a circuit which ended in a timer-plug.

"M'lud . . ." implored Cudlip.

The judge came out of his trance.

"M'lud . . ."

"Yes, Mr Cudlip?"

"I object, m'lud . . ."

"Oh, yes, Mr Cudlip. Sir Francis, kindly rephrase that last question, omitting all reference to the house being set on fire."

The noise in court died away as the judge spoke, but the tension seemed to build up again as March, who had not sat down, again addressed Connal. "Please tell the court why you bought three wooden sugar bowls—replicas of the three shown here—just four days before your wife was burned to death."

Connal did not reply.

After a long pause March said: "You seem disinclined to answer my question. Have you forgotten when you bought the bowls or the purpose for which they were bought?"

Again no reply. In the deep silence, Masters took hold of Green's forearm in a strong grip, warning him to keep quiet and not break the spell by indulging in so much as moving a muscle. Green got the message. He knew that this was the moment Masters had worked for and that it would make or break the Crown case.

"An answer, please, Mr Connal." Sir Francis was timing his requests as skilfully as any great actor his lines.

Counsel again waited in silence. At last Sir Francis turned to the judge. "M'lud, I seem unable to elicit any response from the accused."

Cleghorn frowned. "James Connal, you will answer the question put to you by counsel for the prosecution. Why did you buy three wooden sugar bowls four days before your wife's death?"

There was still no reply from Connal. Masters loosed his grip of Green's arm, as if tacitly to signal that the crisis was over and the victory won.

Cudlip rose. "M'lud," he asked tentatively, "is the question really relevant?"

"The matter of the relevancy of the question does not arise, Mr Cudlip. What is relevant is the wilful refusal of the accused to answer the questions that have been put to him."

"M'lud."

"Yes, Sir Francis?"

"I should like to make sure that your Lordship appreciates not only the relevance but the importance of the unanswered question, and to add that the Crown regards it as the key to the case for the prosecution."

"M'lud," cried Cudlip. "I protest. My learned colleague is bringing an undue and totally unsubstantiated influence to bear on members of the jury."

"Please be quiet, Mr Cudlip. Sir Francis is on his feet. Do you expect him to stand there completely dumb, awaiting the convenience of the accused? If the prosecution has said anything to influence the jury—a fact which I doubt because even Sir Francis' words would not, I suggest, have quite so marked an effect on the jury as the behaviour of the accused—it is because the defence has, by its actions, invited him to do so. The accused is in contempt of court and, as such, cannot claim my protection, only my censure.

Not only are you responsible for his behaviour here, but . . ."

"Like hell he is," whispered Green. "If old Cleggers knew you'd deliberately engineered this, George, he'd have you inside before your feet could touch the ground."

"And you—for aiding and abetting. You're happy enough about it, anyhow."

". . . but," went on the judge, still addressing Cudlip, "I must remind you that, in spite of anything Sir Francis may have said, you are solely responsible for whatever interpretation the members of the jury and I may, either individually or collectively, be forced to accord so wilful a refusal to answer. If you feel the accused needs medical attention, please say so and I can adjourn to let it be given." He then turned to March. "Sir Francis, I trust this will not discomfit you unduly?"

"Not in the least, m'lud, particularly if . . ."

"If what, Sir Francis? What were you about to say?"

"The prosecution would be willing to proceed despite the non-cooperation of the accused if your Lordship would agree to certain alternative arrangements being made."

"Connal's still standing there as large as life," whispered Green. "But I see that bobby has moved very close to the box."

"What sort of alternative arrangements, Sir Francis?"

"If your Lordship would permit me to recall some former witnesses to testify to facts which I would normally have attempted to elicit from the accused himself . . ."

Cudlip, on his feet, said firmly, "M'lud, I really must protest at my learned colleague's suggestion."

"This time, Mr Cudlip, I shall uphold you to the extent that I shall adjourn until after lunch to allow the accused any attention he may need. Please counsel him strongly, Mr Cudlip. Explain that his behaviour will not be tolerated, and then arrange for him to receive any medical attention necessary. You will arrange for a doctor to be brought to the cells as soon as possible. Take the accused down now."

"Thank you, m'lud."

"Meanwhile, I shall want to speak to both counsel on the points of law raised by this situation. Sir Francis, I shall speak to you first, while Mr Cudlip is doing what he has to do. He will join us when he is free to do so."

As the judge rose to go, it seemed to Masters that everybody in court let out a long-pent-up sigh of relief, as though the tourniquet of tension had at last been released and each one could breathe normally again.

CHAPTER VIII

"COVER THE EXHIBIT over," said Masters to Reed, "and see that Mr Hill keeps it under lock and key."

"Not the clerk of the court, Chief? He reckons to hang on to exhibits."

"This was never put into court. But I suspect it will be—later."

"It did its stuff though, didn't it, Chief? It stopped Connal's coughing in church."

Hill joined them. He grinned at Masters. "Satisfied, Chief?"

"More to the point, are you? It's your case, remember."

"Funny thing," said Hill, "I don't feel in the least annoyed that I've been made to look a bit of a Charlie by you and Bill Green. If anybody else had shown me up like you two have, I'd be spitting rust."

"We haven't shown you up. We've helped you. You had enough commonsense to ask for help when it was needed. Proper Charlies don't do that. If they ask at all, it is always too late in the day. I repeat, it is your case, it is not yet concluded, and all the signs point to it going your way. Why should you have any feelings at all, other than to feel pleased at stopping a nasty murderer getting away with his crime?"

"Mr Hill has nailed him, in fact, Chief."

"Not yet. I said stopped and I mean stopped. Getting him convicted will come later if what I think is going to happen actually does so. Now, Reed, away with that bauble and then get yourself some lunch."

"You're not eating, Chief?"

"The D.C.I. and I will have to wait for Sir Francis. So you get yourself fed and watered."

"Right, Chief."

As Reed and Hill carried the exhibit away, Green joined Masters. "Come outside for a smoke, George."

"Good idea."

As they stood by one of the windows in the flagged foyer, exactly where March and Hill had stood on Friday evening, Green asked: "What do you reckon is going on in his muckship's retiring room, George? What points of law are there to discuss?"

"I don't know about points of law, but I think Cleggers will be hauling Frank over the coals."

"What for? He isn't the one who's caused the adjournment."

Masters applied a match to the pipeful of Warlock Flake. "No judge," he said, drawing on the stem to get an even burn, "no judge appreciates conjuring tricks in his court. I reckon he'll tell Frank that whipping away that sheet so dramatically amounted to intimidation of the accused."

"Come off it, George! Intimidation?"

"Connal was struck dumb by the sight of those three bowls and the electrical device. What's that if it isn't intimidation?"

Green grinned. "Nice touch, that. I'm quite proud of having had those bits of element wired up, just for laughs."

"Connal didn't laugh."

"Maybe not. But you were the bloke who thought it all up, so there's no need to be narked."

"Narked? I'm highly delighted. I'm just putting what I think will be the judge's point of view."

"Cleggers caught on though, didn't he?"

"Immediately. And it is just as well he did. If he hadn't realised the importance of that display, he'd have slain Frank in open court."

Reed, who should have gone for lunch, but was still waiting for Hill, had joined them in time to hear this last comment. He asked, "Why, Chief? There was nothing wrong, was there?"

"It would have been almost mandatory for any judge to have done so. It is my belief that Judge Cleghorn—who, quite rightly, is bending over backwards in his efforts to be impartial—has come to exactly the same conclusions as Sir Francis concerning Connal's character. Why shouldn't he? They're both experienced advocates of long standing. They develop a nose for the wrong 'un just as coppers do. Ask the D.C.I. here, and he'll tell you he can scent a real criminal a mile off. I'm talking about habitual, dyed-in-the-wool villains, of course, and not some murderer who, until the time he commits his crime, has led a blameless life."

"There's no aura about the one-off bloke," agreed Green. "The habitual commission of crime, however," he added sententiously, "leaves its mark upon a person in much the same way as any other vocation or job affects the people engaged in it. One of the features of this country is that everybody immediately categorises everybody else by voice, condition of hands, length of hair, whether he carries pens in his pocket, cleans his shoes and so on. By and large we're good at it. Go outside here, now, and I bet I could pick out, for instance, an office worker."

"So could I," said Reed, "but I wouldn't know what job he does in his office."

"Quite right, lad. Nor would I know what specific job any criminal had done."

Reed shrugged his shoulders, and Masters continued. "So, I reckon Cleghorn summed up friend Connal as a plausible rogue and thought him as guilty as hell. But after Connal's performance in the box last Friday afternoon, Cleggers, who can read juries as well as villains, reckoned Connal was by way of being found not guilty. However, as I said, the judge has to be impartial even though, at times, it takes a conscious effort to be so because, like all humans, judges form private opinions."

"We're supposed to be impartial, too, Chief," objected Reed.

"True. But we're not concerned with administering justice. Once we have produced a case establishing a man's guilt—to our own satisfaction—we can forget our impartiality and pull out all the legitimate stops to get him convicted—as we are doing in the case of Connal. But with a chap like Connal a judge has to be extremely careful."

"Why exactly?"

"Cleghorn would bet every penny he had that, if found guilty, Connal will appeal. And the one thing a conscientious judge wants to guard against is a guilty man winning an appeal on a technicality. Appeal judges don't attend trials, they only study proceedings. They look out for technical omissions or commissions. Did the judge instruct the jury fairly? Did he show bias at any time during the trial? If he did err, he would be all right as long as the bias was in favour of the convicted man. But if the bias was against the accused who has been found guilty, the conviction would stand a good chance of being quashed. And so, a judge who is strongly of the opinion that the person being tried is guilty and deserves to be convicted must, in court, appear to be on the side of the guilty one rather than against him. Cleggers knows that he must show no sign of bias against Connal or he will cut the ground from under his own feet by leaving the defence a lever to use in the appeal court."

"But, Chief, because Sir Francis showed those sugar bowls in court, the judge can't be accused of bias against Connal. Cleghorn had absolutely nothing to do with it. He was as surprised as anybody else not in the know."

"Precisely. But it gives him good reason to be a bit tetchy with Sir Francis. All judges like quiet, well-run, undramatic courts. There isn't one who wouldn't view March's little trick with anything but disfavour. Gimmicks of that sort, they believe, are for television drama, not Her Majesty's Courts of Justice. Fortunately for us our display was so immediately illuminating, that Cleghorn realised in a flash the importance of those three bowls and the electrical device. In other words, they proved the case—pictures speaking louder than words, so Cleghorn accepted it—just—without blasting Sir Francis there and then."

"What Sir Francis did wouldn't appear in the transcripts either, Chief."

"True. All the dramatic bit will be lost and, in fact, completely overshadowed by Connal's refusal to answer. That will all be there. The question repeated several times and the judge's warnings. All there."

"I don't agree with you fully," said Green.

"No?"

"About the display being immediately illuminating to the judge. I don't see how it could have been. It hit Connal between the eyes, as it was meant to, but how could Cleghorn have possibly known we had deduced that the fire was started by igniting three wooden bowls of inflammable liquid?"

"He couldn't," admitted Masters. "But he was told in earlier evidence from the Chief Fire Officer that there were three separate and distinct hot spots . . . or do you think I am crediting him with catching on too fast?"

"I dunno," replied Green. "How much does a judge think about these things privately? He hears a lot of evidence. Doesn't he have any private thoughts? I mean, what would Cleghorn be thinking about over the weekend? Wouldn't he be asking himself how it could have been done? Most people would."

"To the point where, given an obvious hint like our exhibit, he would cotton on immediately?"

"Why not? I bet a lot of the blokes in the jury did."

"You could be right. Anyhow, it worked."

"And you," said Green, "engineered it."

"At your instigation."

"Mine? I like that."

"It was you who first said to me that Connal was a nutcase."

"Oh, that!"

"Yes. Oh, that! I'd previously regarded him simply as a bumptious sort of chap, but clever with it. I'd completely overlooked the fact that he could be mad."

"Most murderers are."

"To some degree. But you suggested he was crackers in a clinical sense—as opposed to being temporarily insane or whatever."

"And?"

Masters grimaced. "When I got home on Saturday night—after you'd planted the idea—Wanda said much the same thing as you had done. You two recognised something I'd missed."

"Great minds," murmured Green. "I always told you that girl was the bee's knees, both intellectually and in her character. She could have done so well for herself, too, but she went and married you."

"Pay no attention, Chief," said Reed. "The D.C.I. can't mean what he says because he reckons anything Mrs Masters does is wonderful, and that must even include marrying you."

"Thank you, Reed."

"Shut your trap, laddie," said Green. "Speak when spoken to and, to quote the poets, kindly refrain from putting in your oar."

"Wanda was quite firm about it—dogmatic, almost."

"I'd expect her to be," said Green. "You see, she could put herself in Mrs Connal's shoes. As well as that, she'd sense you were upset about the little boy who died, and that would be too close to home for her. She's got your son, remember, and she's a wise, sensitive lass."

"She told me not to get too involved because Connal is mad. A psychotic, she called him. But I couldn't see why she didn't want me to get too involved."

"She meant emotionally."

"She didn't say so. I got the impression she would have liked me to bow out, if I'd been able to do so."

"So?"

"You and she between you had convinced me I ought to try to play on Connal's madness as dramatically as possible."

"I see. And the solution you eventually came up with involved dropping Frank March right in the fertiliser as far as the judge was concerned."

"It worked, didn't it?"

"Bloody lucky for you it did. But then, I always did say you were jammy. I was telling Wanda and Doris only last week . . ."

Green got no chance to finish his story. The officer of the court—a retired police sergeant—approached them.

"Detective Chief Superintendent Masters, sir?"

"Yes."

"His Lordship would like to see you and a Mr Green in his room, now, sir."

"A Mr Green?" queried the D.C.I. "*The* Mr Green, old timer. Lead the way, friend. And I only hope his Lordship's got some beer in there behind the scenes."

"Only sherry," said the officer with a grimace. "I've never yet had a judge with taste for a decent drink. This way, gentlemen, please."

The judge removed his wig and put it on a stand at the end of the vast desk before moving to the swivel chair.

"I've asked you here alone, because I've got a bone to pick with you, Frank."

March took a chair opposite the judge, pushed his wig back on his head and felt for his cigarettes.

"M'lud?"

"Don't m'lud me," said Cleghorn. "You turned my court into a damned three-ring circus, and I want to know why."

"I should like nothing better than to tell you it all in detail, sir, but that would be highly improper." He offered the judge a cigarette and a light.

"Like that is it?" asked Cleghorn, leaning back and allowing the smoke to trickle from his nostrils. "You feel you can act with impropriety in my court and then suggest it would be improper for me to be told why?"

March carefully tapped a bare fraction of an inch of ash off his cigarette and into the cut-glass tray. "It's this way, sir. The case against Connal was prepared by a comparative tyro—Detective Inspector Hill. And he fell into a trap."

"How come?"

"Connal intended to be tried for murder from the outset. Tried—and acquitted."

The judge sat up, disbelief written on his features.

"You're joking, Frank. No sane man . . ."

"Ah!"

"Ah? What do you mean? Oh, I get it. Sane. You mean Connal was going to plead insanity?"

"No, sir, I don't mean that. I mean that Connal, who appears eminently sane, set out to kill his wife, to be tried for her murder, and acquitted. Hill could never have guessed this. As he was meant to, he saw what appeared to be an easy case against Connal. He was conned into not digging deep. He took what was offered. He was quite satisfied and, to be candid; so was I, that the case was sewn up. Until, that is, I'd had a chance to study Connal and to hear him in the box. I began to have very serious doubts on Friday."

"Doubts? About what?"

"There was a factor Hill hadn't taken into account. The cleverness of the accused. I began to realise just how superficial the Crown case was."

"As prepared by Hill and put by you?"

"Just so, sir. And after Connal had been in the box for a few minutes I could sense the jury swinging away from the Crown to the defence."

"I felt the same, Frank. Cuddles gave him his head and Connal made as good an impression as I've ever encountered from a man on trial for murder."

"But, sir, by this time, I had an overwhelming conviction that Connal was as guilty as hell. . . . To show exactly how I felt, I quoted a bit from one of Bacon's essays, and even Hill got the message."

"Which bit?"

"From 'Of Wisdom for a Man's Self'."

"'It is a poor centre of a man's actions, himself'?"

"Not that, although I took the view that Connal was extremely self-centred. My quote runs, 'It is the nature of extreme self-lovers, as they will set a house on fire, and it were but to roast their eggs.'"

"Apposite." The judge leaned forward to tap the ash from his cigarette. "And put like that . . ." He shook his big head slowly.

"I don't like the idea of a man who has roasted his wife alive getting away with it. Equally, when I'm convinced that a man has been clever enough to hoodwink both the police and myself to the degree where he can virtually build up the case against himself with his own hands, camouflage it to look like a solid edifice, and knock it down when put to the test, then I want more than ever to put a stop to his little games. Indeed, it is my duty to do so, wouldn't you agree?"

"Totally, Frank. But this is a court of law. The accused is innocent until proved guilty to the satisfaction of the jurors. Your personal feelings and convictions are immaterial except in so far as they can be reflected and—even more important—substantiated, during the case you present to those same jurors."

March stubbed out his cigarette. "I knew we had been the

victims of a confidence trick soon after Connal went into the box on Friday. I felt that the police had missed the vital point that would bring the guilt home in the eyes of yourself and the jury."

"What vital point?"

March shrugged. "I didn't know. There was just a glimmering of light in my old mind—it flashed on and off again so quickly that I couldn't identify what it had illuminated. It simply left me with the imprecise knowledge that there was something wrong."

"I guessed so." Cleghorn swivelled his chair and put his feet up on the corner of the desk. "You played for time on Friday afternoon. You kept the milkman in the box for no reason whatsoever."

"No, sir. The milkman's evidence is vital."

"Ah! I missed something, did I? Something you proposed to clear up today?"

"Right, sir. But I confess that I hoped you would rise on Friday evening before I needed to cross-examine Connal."

"To give yourself the weekend to think?"

"To act, sir. I had come to the realisation that Connal was about to make monkeys of us all, but that the traditional conduct of a court would have me hamstrung unless I could persuade you to allow me to recall previous witnesses or, alternatively, unless I could provide the court with enough dramatic testimony to make people start to think again."

"People? Are you referring to me, Frank? To me and the jurors?"

"Actually, sir, I placed the accused at the head of the list. I wanted to make him think. But of course the effort was to be directed at everybody."

"And you thought that a conjuring trick would be the best way to do the job?"

"Not with you, sir. Reasoned verbal argument is obviously the most potent weapon as far as you personally are concerned. But Connal has an ability with words, and unlike you on the bench, is in a position to answer back. By that, I mean, he is capable of taking the sting out of any question I might ask, and is intelligent enough to foresee any line I might be taking and so be ready to forestall me, verbally. But there is no answer to what you are pleased to call a conjuring trick. No answer at all—and Connal's silence proves my point."

The judge opened the cigarette box on the desk and pushed it across for his companion to help himself. "I'm still listening to your . . . what was it you said to butter me up a moment ago? . . . reasoned, verbal argument."

Sir Francis snapped his lighter and leaned across to give the judge a light. "I said I wanted the weekend recess as a period in which to act. Chief Superintendent George Masters of the Yard is a personal friend of mine and, as luck would have it, was D.I. Hill's former chief. So when, on Friday evening, I suggested to Hill that we should ask Masters to give us the benefit of his expertise, there were no local objections. As a result, Masters and D.C.I. Green very kindly gave up their weekend to help us."

"To do what?"

"They read the evidence—the court proceedings. Then they questioned a few people the local police brought in. I assure you, sir, after they'd been at work for a few hours even you wouldn't have recognised the case as the one you are trying. As I said, it would be improper for me to give you all the details, but they gave me a case against Connal. A perfect case. Unfortunately the trial was all but over and to prove what they had given me would, in the normal course of events, have necessitated the recall of certain witnesses."

"And you surmised that having reached the stage where all that remained was for you to cross-examine the accused, I would be unlikely to agree to such a request from you?"

"That had to be my view."

"Quite right. I would have refused."

March spread his hands. "So we had to go for the alternative, sir. We had to produce material evidence in such a way as to shock Connal and—by showing him that we had rumbled his little game—to try to bounce him out of his carapace of self-assurance."

Cleghorn nodded. "I get it. You decided to soften him up by producing a burnt-out typewriter that couldn't be tested. . . ."

"Circumstantial evidence, sir."

"A link, certainly, but a tenuous one."

"To you, sir, perhaps. But I think it made Connal realise we had fathomed his little game."

The judge nodded to show he appreciated the point. March continued: "And then the wooden bowls, sir. We'd got as far as proving he'd bought them."

The judge took his feet from the table and swung round to face March squarely. "And then you proceeded to do your damn conjuring trick. That's what I didn't like, Frank."

"But you saw the importance of it, sir."

"I also saw the effect it had on Connal. Dammit, Frank, you could be accused of doing him grievous bodily harm, right there, under my nose."

"Mental injury, perhaps," corrected March.

"Don't split hairs, Frank. That little show out there was stage-managed with all the skill and dexterity of a music-hall illusionist. And that's not your line of country. Verbal trickery—yes, but prestidigitation—no."

March shrugged as if to show that though he agreed with the judge, even so eminent a member of the Bench could not deny that he, March, had accomplished what he had set out to do.

"Who suggested the pantomime? Masters?"

March stubbed out his cigarette, but did not reply. He was in charge of the way in which the Crown prosecuted the case, and no hint of blame for what had occurred must be laid at Masters' door.

"I saw him there, behind you," said Cleghorn. "And I wondered why. It never occurred to me that he'd been directing you in a music-hall act. I shall want to see him, and his under-strapper, before we return to court."

"The way my case is being presented, sir, is entirely my own responsibility."

"Rubbish, Frank. And don't try to get huffy with me, because I won't wear it. You couldn't have engineered such a show. And I warn you now, when we resume, there's to be no more of it. Understood? It's all very well for Masters. He has a very good name. So good, that his mere presence in court is almost a guarantee of the accused's guilt, because every judge knows that he never brings a charge unless he can substantiate it. His presence out there today is, therefore, an unacceptable invitation to me to favour the Crown. That, however, is not my job. I am expected to be impartial and I intend to be so. I warn you now, Frank, that I shall instruct the jury to ignore what they have seen—to dismiss it from their minds."

"As your Lordship pleases."

"I do please, Frank. And that's the end of it. Now, where is that fellow Cuddles? I want to get on. I'd planned to have this business finished by lunchtime."

"It's getting on for lunchtime now, sir."

"So it is. Time for a sherry, I think, Frank." The judge got to his feet, adjusted the front skirts of his gown which had gone somewhat awry during his recent feet-up, and moved across to a wall cupboard. "Tio Pepe or La Ina?"

It was while the judge was pouring the drinks that the officer announced Cudlip, and defence counsel flustered into the room.

"Ah, there you are, Cuddles. What news?"

"The doctor wishes to remove my client to hospital, m'lud."

"He what?" asked March excitedly.

"Why? What's wrong with him?" asked Cleghorn.

"The doctor cannot be sure, m'lud. He suspects aphasia."

"When will he know for certain?"

"He has called an ambulance, m'lud, but is waiting for your permission to remove him from the court."

"Really? Here, have a glass of sherry, Cuddles, while I think about this."

Cudlip accepted La Ina.

"Is Connal speaking yet?"

"No, m'lud. He is incapable of speech."

"What is aphasia exactly? Total loss of the speech faculty?"

"That is my understanding, m'lud."

"And that's what the doctor has diagnosed?"

"Not exactly, m'lud. He thinks it is aphasia, but he says there will have to be confirmatory tests carried out at the hospital."

"And if I refuse permission for him to leave his cell?"

"You can't, sir, can you?" asked March hopefully. "If the man is ill . . ."

164

"You keep out of this, Frank. Dammit, you're responsible for his condition."

March got to his feet. "I cannot accept that, sir. What exactly are you accusing me of doing or causing to be done to the accused?"

"Come off it, Frank. You know you're responsible for administering the shock or whatever it is that brings on aphasia."

March shook his head. "I still won't admit to that, sir. Whatever caused this trouble must have been latent in the accused. The mere sight of three sugar bowls wouldn't have caused an innocent party any alarm, because he wouldn't have recognised the significance of them."

"M'lud," protested Cudlip. "The Crown is getting away with murder. . . ."

"Not the Crown; Connal," said March.

Cudlip shrugged in despair. "May Connal go, sir? The doctor is waiting for your agreement."

"He can go," growled Cleghorn. "I would be in the wrong to deny him necessary medical treatment, and we can't proceed if the fellow can't speak."

"Thank you, sir. I'll just go and . . ." Cudlip scuttled towards the door.

"Cuddles," called the judge. "Tell the doctor I want to know—as soon as he arrives at the hospital—how long it will be before Connal can be brought back here."

"M'lud."

"What a bloody mess!" snorted Cleghorn after defending counsel had gone. He moved to the fireplace and pushed the bell to summon the officer. When the officer appeared, Cleghorn said to him. "Please inform the clerk that the court has risen for lunch and that I hope to resume at two-thirty. And also tell Detective Chief Superintendent Masters and a Mr Green who is with him that I would like to see them here, now, please."

"Masters," growled Cleghorn, before the Chief Superintendent and Green were fairly inside the room, "what the devil do you mean—or hope to achieve—by turning my court into a bad imitation of a third-rate vaudeville show?"

Masters took his time. Still standing between the desk and the door he said, quietly: "I wasn't aware that I had done so, m'lud. But as I assume you are referring to the effect the sudden disclosure of the three wooden bowls had on Connal, then I would call the incident a dramatic success, where dramatic has connotations other than those generally associated with popular theatre. Perhaps impressive would be a better word, as we sought to impress your Lordship and the jury as well as to encourage the accused into the exaggerated behaviour he displayed."

"Good God," stormed Cleghorn. "Are you telling me you stage-managed that charade with the intention of causing the man to succumb to aphasia?"

"Not aphasia, m'lud," said Masters quietly. "I think you will find that after the psychiatrists have done a few tests they will rule out aphasia."

"I see. You're an expert on these conditions?"

"I have been reading them up recently, sir," confessed Masters.

"That's right, m'lud," said Green. "The Chief Superintendent has been making a special study of psycho-ceramics."

"Psycho-cer . . ." The judge looked from one detective to the other. "Psycho-ceramics? Ceramics are something to do with pottery."

"That's right, m'lud," said Green gravely. "Psycho-ceramics are crackpots. Nutcases if you prefer it."

Sir Francis covered his mouth with his hand. Masters took a sudden interest in the ceiling. Then the judge grinned. "I like your style," he said to Green. "Crackpots! Here, gentlemen, have a glass of sherry. And while I'm getting it, young Masters, you can start explaining yourself. And don't try to put anything over on me. I've admired the clarity with which you have given evidence in court on the few occasions you've appeared when I've been presiding. So keep it clear and factual this time. You say the accused is not suffering from aphasia, but that whatever it is he is suffering from, you brought about by a calculated display that could earn you membership of the Magic Circle?"

"Right," agreed Green, accepting his sherry.

"Masters?"

"Aphasia, m'lud, is the loss or impairment of the capacity to use words as symbols of ideas, as I suppose you already appreciate."

Cleghorn nodded. "Struck dumb, in other words."

"But," went on Masters, "aphasia is organic; that is, it is a malfunction of certain organs of the living body."

"You mean damage to the brain, don't you?"

"Quite, m'lud. The damage in aphasia is caused by lesions in the cortex and association paths in the brain. It is not a defect in the simple mechanics of speaking."

"You mean it is an injury to the brain which causes impairment of thought?"

"Exactly, m'lud. Aphasia is mental and not physical. But—and this is probably where the doctor who was called in was misled—hysterical speech defects may imitate the symptoms of aphasia."

"Hysterical?" queried the judge.

"Yes, m'lud. Not quite in the popular sense—hysterical people requiring a slap to quieten them."

"Go on."

"Hysteria, m'lud, is a condition in which the symptoms or signs of illness are reproduced by a patient for some purpose advantageous to himself without his being fully aware of his motive in doing so."

"Sounds like scrimshanking to me," grumbled Green.

Masters shook his head. "The malingerer deliberately and consciously simulates illness for some purpose. The hysteric is unaware of his motives. This is what distinguishes between the two."

"Am I right in supposing then," said Cleghorn, "that where the scrimshanker—to use Green's earthy word—is usually unable to maintain the fiction under questioning and clever medical examination, the hysteric can and does do so?"

"Right, sir, except that on occasions I suspect it is quite difficult to determine where hysteria ends and malingering begins."

"I see."

Before the judge could phrase the next question that he was

plainly intent on asking, Cudlip returned to the room.

"Got him away, Cuddles?"

"Yes, m'lud. The doctor will call the court office as soon as there is any news."

"Fine. You know Chief Superintendent Masters and Mr Green, I imagine?"

"By repute only, m'lud. I've never had the pleasure of either conducting or opposing one of their cases."

"You have now. Sit down and listen and you'll learn a thing or two. Masters here says Connal is not suffering from aphasia but from hysteria, which very conveniently cropped up for him just at a tricky moment."

"I would prefer to wait for the professional medical verdict, m'lud."

"Of course you would, Cuddles. But until we get it, we may as well hear Masters' thoughts on the matter. Then, at least, we'll not be entirely in the dark when the quacks pronounce."

"I suppose I shall be allowed to mention diminished responsibility?" asked Cudlip.

"Not after the show your man put up on Friday," said Sir Francis. "He was in full control then."

"What do you think, Masters?" asked Cleghorn.

"I'd better repeat for Mr Cudlip's sake that the term hysteria is frequently misapplied to histrionic or uncontrolled behaviour, whereas it should be reserved for psychogenic conditions having a motive of gain."

"Ah!" said Sir Francis. "Gain, eh? Advantage of any sort, I suppose?"

Masters nodded.

"But, psychogenic. . . ?" queried Cudlip. "Surely that means there is a psychosis—a mental disorder—present?"

"No, Mr Cudlip," countered Masters. "Psychogenesis is the development of mental characteristics—the process by which activities or ideas originate in the mind or psyche. We all of us undergo it, all our lives."

"When you say gain," persisted Cudlip, "what are you implying, Mr Masters?"

"The development of hysteria, Mr Cudlip, is usually understood as enabling the person who evinces the symptoms to escape from a difficult situation."

"Such as finding himself rumbled this morning when he got into the witness box," said March.

"Frank!" said Cleghorn sharply. "That was presumptuous and entirely unwarranted."

"Sorry, sir."

"Don't worry, Cuddles. The court can only act on specialist medical opinion. But we'd better hear Masters out, because he certainly seems to be speaking with authority, even though it is entirely off the record and just for our benefit."

Cudlip seemed unhappy, but he nodded his agreement. Green offered him a Kensitas. "Cheer up, Mr Cudlip. Even if what my pal has to say has no relevance to this case, it will be useful knowledge for future cases."

"Yes, yes, I suppose so."

"Oh, it will. You could bring it in at any time. I can remember a quote from one of the papers His Nibs has been reading up. It says that hysteria is protean in manifestation and may simulate any disease. 'Protean' is a new one on me, but George says it merely means taking on many shapes. In other words you could drag it in at any time to baffle technical witnesses. Remember that question in the Rouse case—what is the co-efficient of expansion of brass? It demolished the evidence of the bloke who couldn't come up with the answer."

Cudlip nodded. Cleghorn said: "Tell me, Masters, there must be a predisposition to hysteria, mustn't there?"

"Of course, m'lud. Hysterical bouts may cover a short period of the life of the person manifesting them, or they may cover a large part. But almost invariably they seem to affect a person's weak point. Thus a telephonist may get a bout of hysterical deafness . . ."

"I see. But anybody else may suffer if they are obsessed by a desire not to hear something—such as bad news?"

"You've got it, sir. Any of the senses can be affected in much the same way. A person with very poor sight could develop hysterical blindness or somebody who didn't want to see something—even though their eyesight was perfect—could develop the same symptoms. But I think I should remind you, m'lud, and Mr Cudlip, that hysterical amnesia is not accepted in law as mental illness."

"Neither is it, by jove! That's a point worth remembering, Cuddles," said Cleghorn. "I'd forgotten that."

Cudlip nodded unhappily.

"To get back to the question of predisposition," said Masters, addressing Cleghorn. "The offensively self-conceited or self-assertive person may be your hysteric. I say may be, because not all of them are . . ."

"You mean those who really have cause to be fond of themselves may not be potential hysterics?"

"Cause, sir? Is there ever cause for that sort of behaviour? But you are right. If an achiever has a tip about himself, then one can see reason for it, however distasteful one finds such an attitude."

"I get the point."

"The buffs say environment is of great moment in producing the hysterical personality. Data show that minor injuries at work or on the road readily produce hysteria, because such injuries often carry compensation. But the same injuries on a rugger field or in the home rarely cause hysterical reactions because there is no likelihood of compensation."

"Good heavens," said Cleghorn, "what have we come to! You know, without ever having seen this in print, I had come to much the same conclusion myself."

"So it's not the old cry of a deprived childhood that produces them?" asked March.

"Not deprived, Frank, but bad management by parents in the formative years does give rise to it. What happens is that the dreams and ideas of normal childhood are exaggerated by the years that pass and so are prolonged into adult life."

"You mean they never grow up," growled Green.

"Roughly that. In childhood the dividing line between reality and make-believe is not all that clear-cut. A child can easily think he is a cowboy fighting Indians whilst helping his mother to hang out the washing on the line."

"We all did that."

"So we did, as children. But with some kids—those whose parents make reality too unpleasant for the child—this business of escaping into the world of imagination is exaggerated."

"As a sort of defence?" asked Cudlip. "Just as adults seek to escape through drink, perhaps?"

"Very much like that. But if the child in question is astute enough to learn that by retreating into the world of simulation there is an advantage to be gained, then he is certainly developing an hysterical personality."

"Explain, please," requested the judge.

"The most common symptom with this type of child who doesn't like school, is to say that he feels sick at the start of a new term; but if his mother keeps him at home, he'll eat a hearty meal."

The judge grunted. "What happens to the same child as he grows older?"

"Naturally, as he gets up in years, he can accept the realities of life more readily. The world of make-believe recedes, but it is never pushed away completely."

"Ah! You are about to say that if the management of this older child is . . . how shall I put it? . . . still injudicious? . . . and that if, as a result, the realities of life—or the environment, if you like— remain harsh, then the normal acceptance of reality is arrested?"

"That's it, m'lud. The tendency to escape from reality by what the medics call subconscious simulation becomes ingrained and then you have a life-long potential hysteric on your hands."

"You deserve more sherry for that little exposition, Masters. Pass your glass—all of you, more sherry?"

"I don't like this, sir," said Cudlip.

"Don't like La Ina, Cuddles? Where's your palate, man? Oh, very well, change to Tio Pepe. Will the same glass do?"

"Not the sherry," expostulated Cudlip. "The discussion."

"Oh? Why not?" queried the judge. "I'm rather enjoying it. I can think of few better ways of spending a period of enforced idleness than to sit with a glass of sherry and to listen to so craggy a disquisition as the one Masters is treating us to. I must say that though I have always had a great regard for our police, I had never realised that individual members went to such lengths in their reading. I am reliably informed, Cuddles, that Masters here is one of our leading experts in psycho-ceramics."

"Is he indeed, sir?" said Cudlip, totally unaware of the smirks and grins that accompanied his unthinking acceptance of the judge's words. "What I don't like is that we should be here, discussing the case, before it is finished. It is improper, sir, if I may be allowed to say so."

"Who is discussing a case?" asked Cleghorn.

"We are."

"Have you heard the case mentioned?"

"Not exactly."

"Cuddles," said the judge indulgently, "nothing has been said about the case except when I had Frank in here alone to tell him how much I disapproved of his behaviour. But tell me this. Had your client collapsed in the witness box due to—shall we say—pneumonia, would you raise any objection if, during the enforced recess, I discussed pneumonia with other people?"

"No, of course not."

"Your client—you tell us—is suffering from aphasia."

"So the doctor told me."

"Why then should I not learn something about aphasia, with no bias against your client?"

"Put that way, m'lud . . ."

"Thank you, Cuddles. But you must appreciate that for some time now we have been discussing a different complaint—hysteria. If your client is suffering from aphasia, how in the name of all that's holy can you raise objections to our discussing hysteria?"

Cudlip looked abashed and took a sip at the Tio Pepe the judge had given him in place of the former La Ina.

"So now we can continue," said Cleghorn. "Carry on, Masters."

"When the child that is predisposed to hysteria grows up," said Masters, "his personality is characterised by a great tendency to react excessively to situations and surroundings—like an actor playing a part."

"Does that mean," demanded the judge, "that he would react to an insult by doing violence?"

172

"It could well be, sir. The reaction becomes so habitual that our hysteric sees nothing wrong in outrageous behaviour. And—though I must mention no name at the moment, sir—I would like you to appreciate that the hysteric's over-reaction is the basis of an undue suggestibility in these people."

"How come?" demanded Green.

"Suggestions, which can be either deliberate or inadvertent—not necessarily by words but by gestures or actions—"

"Like conjuring tricks?" murmured Green.

Masters ignored him and carried on.

"—are subconsciously accepted by the hysteric and, as a consequence, are subconsciously acted upon."

"They don't know they're doing it?" asked Cleghorn.

"Don't know *why* they are doing it," corrected Masters.

"Sorry. Go on."

"So, sir, when the hysteric suddenly finds himself in a tricky situation—dangerous, if you like—the harsh, unavoidable consequences of which he cannot face, he immediately excludes it from his consciousness and escapes from the situation by employing one of his hysterical symptoms."

"Which can be blindness, deafness, dumbness?"

"Or other things, sir, I believe—like a refusal to move limbs, or even fighting off anybody who approaches."

Cleghorn nodded. "So he can swing from one extreme to the other. From paralysis to bellicose attitudes?"

"Precisely, sir. I think I'm right in saying that there is no actual physical attitude or clinical disability which may not—seemingly—be paralleled by the hysteric."

Cleghorn grunted. He turned to Cudlip. "Are you finding this interesting, Cuddles?"

"No, m'lud."

"Frank?"

"Yes, m'lud."

"A divergence of opinion. What's the answer, Masters?"

"To the clinical problem, sir, or the legal one?"

"Leave the legal one to me."

"Of course. I suppose the clinical answer must lie first in correct diagnosis which can be most difficult, I understand."

"Why? You claim to have diagnosed it easily enough."

"No, sir. I didn't diagnose it, I had to assume it for the reasons you know. I could easily have been wrong, in which case certain steps we took would have been abortive."

"I'll accept that. What next?"

"After diagnosis, the medics would have to discover what are the situations the hysteric wishes to avoid. . . ."

"Which you think you've done?"

"Just so, sir. After that . . . well, the treatment would be up to the head-shrinker responsible for him. I'm no psychiatrist . . ."

"Modesty will get you anywhere," said Green. "And he's got the audience to prove it."

"There's just one point I should add, sir," said Masters, ignoring the interruption. "I believe that hysterical fits never occur when the person is alone, and always happen as a reaction to a situation that is emotionally important."

"And that's the lot?" asked Sir Francis.

"Isn't it enough?" demanded Green.

Masters looked at the judge. "We have been avoiding cases, sir . . ."

"Yes?"

"The big thing about hysterics is that they are always intent on impressing others."

"Like impressing juries?" asked Sir Francis.

Masters didn't reply.

The judge rang for his clerk.

"Ring the hospital, please, Mr Adams. Ask for definite news of Connal."

"Yes, m'lud. But in anticipation of a long delay, I have been seeing how best to rejig your list."

"Excellent."

Adams was back very quickly.

"I have been asked to tell you, m'lud, that the hospital cannot say how long they will need to keep the prisoner. They say they have diagnosed hysteria, m'lud, and that such a condition may resolve itself quite quickly, or may take weeks to treat."